LASSIE
Forbidden Valley

LASSIE
Forbidden Valley

Doris Schroeder

A TARGET BOOK

published by
the Paperback Division of
W. H. ALLEN & Co. Ltd

A Target Book
Published in 1978
by the Paperback Division of W. H. Allen & Co. Ltd.
A Howard & Wyndham Company
44 Hill Street, London W1X 8LB

First published in 1959 in the U.S.A.
by Western Publishing Company, Inc.

Printed in Great Britain by
Hunt Barnard Printing Ltd, Aylesbury, Bucks.

ISBN 0 426 20022 5

Contents

1

A Birthday

It had been raining hard during the night, but when Timmy opened one eye to peek out the window, the sun was streaming in so brightly that it made him blink. He sat up in bed, rubbing his eyes hard and wondering sleepily what had made him wake up on this very first day of spring vacation.

Then he heard a scratching at the door and soft little whimpers. Lassie!

Timmy piled out of bed in a hurry and ran to open the door. Sure enough, there she sat waiting, her beautiful plume of a tail waving from side to side.

'Hi!' Timmy gave the handsome collie a hug, and laid his cheek against her soft white ruff for a moment. 'I'm sorry the door was closed. It wasn't supposed to be, but I guess the wind blew it shut last night in the storm.'

Lassie touched his cheek with her soft nose, in a most

forgiving gesture. Then she picked up a small square package that was lying beside her on the floor in the hallway. It was tied with a red, white, and blue ribbon.

'What's that?' Timmy asked, holding out his hand.

Lassie put the package into his hand, and then barked joyfully, as if to say, 'Open it and we'll both have a look!'

Timmy sat down on the floor, staring at the package, his face breaking into a happy grin. He had completely forgotten that today was his birthday! 'Golly! Thanks, Lassie! A birthday present!'

He gasped as he took the cover off the box inside. 'Lassie! Look! Mum got it for me! It's a fishing reel! Just like Dad's, only smaller!'

Lassie danced around barking excitedly as Timmy dashed into the kitchen where Ruth Martin, his adopted mother, was cooking breakfast.

'Mum! Golly! Thanks a lot! You remembered!' He ran to her, waving the present in his hand.

Ruth turned from the big old cookstove and held out her arms. 'Happy birthday, dear!' She caught him in a big hug. 'I hope you like it. Dad picked it out because it was the same kind as his, and he heard you say you'd like to have it.'

'It's sure swell!' Timmy's eyes danced. 'Wait till Boomer gets a look! I bet I catch a real big fish with this!'

Ruth smiled. 'I bet you will!'

'Mum!' Timmy was already pulling in a humdinger of a trout, in his lively mind. 'How soon can Dad 'tach it to my fishing rod?'

'Why, I think he might manage to do it when he comes in to breakfast. That is, if you're all washed up and ready to have breakfast with him.'

'Come on, Lassie!' Timmy ran for the hall door. 'I'll be back fast, Mum. Take care of my reel!' Then he was gone, and Ruth heard him run down the hall, Lassie barking at his heels.

Ruth Martin smiled happily at the memory of Timmy's bright face. He had been a timid, strange little six-year-old when he first came to live with them. He had lived in other foster homes since his parents died, and he hadn't expected to find a real home and affection here.

But when they had legally adopted him the first moment it was possible to arrange it, he had blossomed out. Now he was so much a part of their lives and their hearts that it almost seemed as if he had always been with them.

Lassie had had a lot to do with it, Ruth had to admit to herself. It was the gentle, intelligent big collie that had first won the orphan boy's confidence. They were pals after the first minute that they met. And they were always together. Lassie could be counted on to keep her young master out of danger, if not out of mischief!

Uncle Petrie, who was Paul's uncle and lived with them, helping with the chores, had a lot to do with Timmy's happy life there. He was never too busy to stop and chat with the youngster. He had an answer to all Timmy's questions, on everything from planting corn to explaining thunderstorms. And usually he was right. Timmy thought Uncle Petrie was just about the smartest person in the world, next to Mum and Dad Martin.

Yes, Timmy was a happy boy. And they were happy to have him.

The small farm was no rich estate, and it took hard work to keep it going. But the Martins wouldn't have changed it for the biggest ranch in the world if it had meant giving up Timmy.

Ruth had told Timmy this, the day he had come home from school with traces of tears on his cheeks and some of the old fears in his eyes. One of the older boys had jeered at him because he was 'only an adopted kid'.

She had put her arm around Timmy's thin little shoulders and hugged him tightly, while she reassured him that she and his dad loved him just as much as if he had been their own flesh and blood. 'You see, dear,' she had gone on gravely, 'other folks have to take the children that the good Lord sends them and be satisfied. They can't pick the little boy or girl they'd most like to have in their family, but your dad and I had the chance to choose the one we wanted, out of the whole world. And it was *you!*'

'Golly!' Timmy had breathed, happiness again in his grin. 'Wait'll I tell that big guy!'

And there had been no shadow since.

Timmy's best friend, next to Lassie who was special, was Boomer Bates. Whatever mix-ups and mischief Timmy didn't find his way into and out of again, Boomer could be depended on to get them both into. They were almost the same age, within a couple of weeks.

Thinking of some of their pranks, Ruth Martin was chuckling to herself as Paul came in from his barn chores to wash up for breakfast. He saw the birthday present unwrapped on the table. 'Ah ha!' he grinned. 'I see he found it!'

'You mean *Lassie* found it and took it to him! All I

had to do was show it to her and say, "This is for Timmy!" and she had it and was on her way to wake him up.'

'How did he like it?' Paul asked through the soap-suds.

'You'll hear any second!' she laughed, as Lassie made a sudden appearance in the hall doorway. 'Here's the advance guard coming in to report!'

Lassie said, 'Wroof!' and Timmy hurried in, hair and face shining.

'Happy birthday, skipper!' Paul greeted him from the sink, as he finished drying his hands.

Timmy hurried to the table, and was picking up the fishing reel as if it were solid gold set with diamonds and rubies. 'It's just what I wanted, Dad. The very one we saw in Colton's window. You remembered!'

'Sure, son! I didn't dare forget it, after the way you talked about it all afternoon!' Paul's eyes twinkled, and he came to the table and put his arm across Timmy's shoulders.

'Will you 'tach it for me, Dad?' Timmy asked eagerly.

'Right after breakfast!' Paul promised, drawing up his chair. 'And I see we're having some special blue-berry pancakes today. Your mum is really celebrating!'

Breakfast was on the table when Uncle Petrie came in. He was holding something behind his back and look-ing very mysterious.

'Morning, Uncle Petrie!' Timmy stretched his neck to see what Uncle Petrie was hiding, but Uncle Petrie turned a little, just far enough to keep it out of sight.

'Mornin',' Uncle Petrie answered gruffly, and sat down. He still kept one hand out of range of Timmy's eyes. Timmy waited impatiently as Ruth set a plateful

11

of hot cakes in front of Uncle Petrie. Wasn't Uncle Petrie going to say 'Happy Birthday' or something?

'Kinda brisk wind a-blowin' this morning,' Uncle Petrie remarked casually. 'Whippin' away the tail end of that storm.'

'Good weather for ploughing,' Paul nodded. 'We'd better get to work first thing on that west field.'

'Got to check the oil first. That plough's been actin' a mite sluggish.' Whatever Uncle Petrie had been carrying in his hand, he had put it down on the floor beside him and was picking up his knife and fork. Timmy was beginning to think that it wasn't a birthday present, after all. He felt hurt and disappointed.

'Eat your cakes, son,' Ruth smiled.

Timmy lifted his fork towards his mouth, and then put it down. He couldn't stand the suspense any more. 'Uncle Petrie,' he began in a small voice, 'look what Dad just gave me *for my birthday*.' He held up the reel.

Uncle Petrie laid aside his knife and fork and looked astonished. 'Birthday? You havin' a birthday?' His eyes twinkled mischievously. 'Think of that! Why didn't you tell me about it?'

'B-But I did!' Timmy's eyes were wide. 'Yesterday — an' the day before! Don't you 'member?'

'Hmm!' Uncle Petrie frowned and pulled at his ear. 'Wait now! Seems to me I do remember somebody sayin' somethin' about a birthday.'

'It was me! I told you!' Timmy's lower lip quivered.

'Oh, yes! Now I rec'lect!' Uncle Petrie nodded and grinned. He reached down beside his chair and came up with the package he had been hiding. It was a small telescope that he had bought over a month ago for this very occasion. 'Now I wonder what this thing might be.'

12

He shook the package and studied it, while Timmy's eyes grew rounder and rounder. Then Uncle Petrie held out the package to Timmy, across the table. 'Maybe you better take a look!'

Timmy gave a delighted chuckle as he reached for it, and started tearing the wrapping paper off it so fast that Paul called out, 'Hey, take it easy, butch! It won't melt before you see what it is!' But Paul and Ruth and Uncle Petrie were all smiling happily at Timmy's excitement.

Timmy was speechless for a moment as he gazed on the one other thing besides the reel that he had been longing for. When he found his tongue again, he told Uncle Petrie, who sat beaming at him, 'Thanks! Thanks a million, Uncle Petrie! It's sure keen!'

'Now you and I can climb to the top of Old Blue some day soon and see how far you can look with it!' Paul promised.

'Wow!' There was real delight in Timmy's voice. 'Now I've got a fishin' reel and a spyglass. I guess there's just about nothin' more I want!'

'Except to finish your breakfast before those hot cakes get cold!' Ruth laughed.

And Timmy, with the fishing reel at one side of his plate and the telescope at the other, managed to eat the cakes in record time. He even finished a small helping of bacon and scrambled eggs to top off the meal, while his dad was attaching the reel to Timmy's small fishing pole.

'Mum!' Timmy's round face was flushed and eager. 'Can me an' Boomer go fishin' this morning?'

'Boomer and I, dear,' she corrected gently.

'You?' Timmy looked puzzled. 'Fishin'?'

Ruth laughed. 'No, honey. I meant you should say "Boomer and I" not "me and Boomer."' Then she glanced over at Paul to see how he felt about Timmy and Boomer going on a fishing expedition – he might have made some plans for Timmy. She caught Paul's eye and lifted one eyebrow questioningly.

Paul smiled and nodded. 'I guess there's no reason why they can't go, Ruth. Especially when there's a new fishing reel to try out. And a telescope!'

'Whee! Wait'll Boomer sees them!' Timmy was on his feet, grinning from ear to ear. 'Can I go right away?'

'I'd better phone Boomer's mother, so he'll be through his chores when you get there. And there's a little job of feeding the hens here, and some eggs to collect.'

'I'll take care of it right off!' Timmy sped towards the door. But quick as he was, Lassie was there before him, barking excitedly and prancing around. Timmy dashed out, with Lassie at his heels, and the screen door slammed. A moment later, Timmy's head popped in again. 'I'm sorry, Mum. I didn't mean to let it go so hard!' Then he was gone again, but this time he made sure the door closed softly behind him.

'You'll teach that wild Indian some manners yet!' Uncle Petrie chuckled.

Ruth laughed and went to the telephone.

Boomer's mother, Mrs Bates, was slow coming to the phone, and when she found out who was at the other end, she exclaimed, 'Ruth Martin! I'm glad you called. I was just telling Dr Wilson that I'd better call you up and warn you!'

Ruth gasped. 'The doctor? Warn me of what?'

'Boomer came down with pink spots and a high fever last night, and Doc's quite sure it's the measles. How's

14

your boy? Has he started them yet?' Mrs Bates rattled off her question.

'Why, no! He seems all right so far! But I'll check him right away!' Ruth told her.

They chatted a moment more and then Ruth hung up and turned to Paul. 'Now it's measles. Had we better keep Timmy home today?'

Timmy and Lassie were coming in with the egg basket, and Timmy heard the end of the question. 'Mum!' he stopped in the doorway, looking stricken. 'Why?'

Ruth hurried to him and turned him around so that the sunlight fell on his face. There were no pink spots. Her hand went to his forehead. Cool and normal. No fever.

'What's the matter, Mum?'

'Boomer's mother thinks he's coming down with measles. Do you feel all right, dear?' she asked anxiously.

'Why sure!' Timmy's forehead wrinkled. 'What's measles?'

'It's a fever. You feel hot and you have to stay in bed for a few days, and you get pink spots all over you.'

Timmy looked critically at his bare arms. 'I don't have any spots.' He sounded a little disappointed.

'You don't have a fever, either.' Ruth was relieved. Maybe the measles were going to skip Timmy.

'Do I have to stay home, then?' Timmy looked wistful. Paul and Ruth Martin exchanged questioning looks. Paul frowned. 'You don't want to go fishing all by yourself, do you?'

'But I won't be all by myself!' Timmy put his arm around Lassie. 'Lassie'll be with me. She loves to fish.'

15

'Well . . . ' Paul hesitated.

Ruth held out only a moment more, then, 'All right, Timmy. You may go, but you must promise to be home before the sun's behind the hills. And, Lassie, you take good care of him, do you hear?'

Lassie barked and her plume waved excitedly. Then she took Timmy's sleeve between her teeth and started to pull him towards the door.

'Whoa, girl!' Ruth laughed. 'Don't you two want me to fix you a picnic lunch?'

Lassie let go of Timmy's sleeve and went racing to the shelf where Timmy's lunch box was kept. She stretched herself up tall on her hind legs, and plucked the lunch box off the shelf, by its handle. She trotted over to the sink with it and set it up on the drain board where Ruth usually packed Timmy's lunch on school days. Then she backed off, turned and barked loudly at Ruth as if she were saying, 'I've done my part. Now *you* get to work!'

All three of them laughed, and Ruth told Lassie, 'Okay! I can take a hint!' And she went over and started fixing up a tasty lunch and putting everything into it that she knew Timmy liked. And she didn't forget a meaty bone for Lassie.

A few minutes later, Paul and Ruth Martin stood in the front yard of the little farmhouse, and watched two figures disappear up the road.

'I hope he'll be careful,' Ruth sighed. 'The creek bank may be slippery after last night's storm.'

'Don't worry,' Paul told her with a smile, 'Lassie'll see that nothing happens to him!'

2

Forbidden Ground

It was pretty close to half a mile from the Martin farm before the woods began. At first, the trees were sort of scattered, and there were a lot of stumps to show where the Calverton settlers had cut the wood for their houses a long time ago. But as Timmy and Lassie made their way deeper into the woods, the trees were thicker, and so close together at some places that it was quite dark under them.

He just kept on going towards Willow Creek, and Lassie trotted right along with him, sometimes running ahead and sniffing the ground as if she wanted to be sure there was nothing dangerous waiting for Timmy. Other times, she kept very close to his side, especially when there were little crackling noises in the brush. She was careful to stay between him and the noises, and now and then she would sort of growl under her breath as she stared at the bushes. When she did that, Timmy

2

would swallow hard and hurry a little till they were well past the danger spot. But he never did catch a glimpse of anything except once a grey squirrel scampered up a tree trunk not five feet away, and chattered angrily at both him and Lassie.

Timmy's favourite fishing spot was in bright sunlight by the time he and Lassie arrived. He had a small can of worms in his pocket for baiting the hook, and he chose the fattest one for his first try. 'Got to have a big worm for a big fish,' he told Lassie, but Lassie was more interested in trying to catch some very tiny minnows swimming in a little pool filled up by the rain.

Things were very wet, and the creek bank was muddy and slippery. Timmy cast his line well out into the middle of the creek, and a couple of minutes later, the reel was singing as something carried the hook along swiftly through the rain-swollen stream. The rod jerked and bent.

Timmy hung on to the fishing rod and yelled with excitement. When the pull continued, he tried to 'play' the unseen fish, and reel it in a little at a time.

Lassie had given up her minnow-chasing and was standing up on the bank, watching as Timmy struggled to pull in his catch. Suddenly Timmy's feet slipped on the muddy slope, and he started to fall backward. The fishing rod was jerked out of his hands by the pull of the rushing creek, and flew out into the middle of the stream.

By the time Timmy had scrambled, mud-caked, to his feet again, the rod and precious reel were out of sight, carried away by the swift current. They came into sight again just once, as the water tossed them against a rock in mid-stream. Then they were swallowed up.

Timmy didn't stop to think. He started down the bank towards the water, slipping and sliding in the mud. But before he could reach the edge of the creek, Lassie had made a long leap from the top of the bank, and grabbed hold of him by his belt.

Timmy was pulled off his feet, but he tried to scramble up and tear himself loose. 'Let go, Lassie! I got to bring back my rod an' reel!' But Lassie held on.

Timmy gave up, and sat down in the mud. He had a hard time fighting back his tears, and Lassie poked a comforting nose against his cheek. Timmy slipped his arm over her neck and rested his head against her white ruff. 'Okay, Lassie. I guess you were right. There was no use tryin'. But it was my brand-new birthday present.' He choked back a small sob.

Lassie whined sympathetically and they sat leaning against each other for a couple of minutes, both caked with mud.

Timmy stood up and tried to brush the sticky mud off his corduroys. But now a brisk spring breeze had come up and was sweeping through the woods and making him shiver.

'Guess we better find some place out of the wind, where I can dry off,' he told Lassie, and looked around for it.

His face brightened as he saw the familiar long slope of Old Blue Top, not over a hundred yards away. The sun was beating down on the lush green grass of the hill-side, and the breeze up there seemed to be gentler than down in the woods, as it moved the grass in long slow waves. 'Come on, Lassie!' He started off, lunch box in one hand and the telescope in his other. 'We'll climb to the top an' look down at the haunted house. I bet we'll see lots of things with our new telescope!'

But Lassie stood her ground and barked at him. Timmy went a few feet, and then noticed that she wasn't following.

'I'm not going near the house, honest!' he assured her, impatiently. 'I promised Dad I wouldn't, and I'm not going to. So come on. We can look through the spyglass, 'thout breaking our promise!'

Lassie hesitated, her head tilted to one side as if she were thinking it over. She whimpered a little, uneasily.

'Aw, come on!' Timmy urged. '*I'm* goin', anyhow!' And he set out for the hillside. Lassie hesitated for a second till she saw that he was going ahead without her, and then she gave up and went bounding after him.

And for the whole long hike up the slope of Calverton County's longest and tallest hill, she stayed close by her small owner's side, her eyes alert for possible danger, and her sensitive nose sniffing cautiously for threatening scents.

Timmy was tired, but quite dried off by the time they reached the tall old oak tree that topped the hill. An old rail fence marked the boundary of the Brunson farm down in the valley below. Timmy sat down on a flat rock close by the fence and caught his breath, while Lassie stretched out close beside him.

The last time Timmy had been up here was way last autumn. He and Boomer had been exploring the hill, and had sat down to rest right here. They had been surprised, as they peered down through the old fence, to see a boarded-up house down there, and old weathered farm buildings without a sign of life around them.

Timmy, as a newcomer to Calverton, had no idea whose place it was, but Boomer had. 'It's the haunted house!' he had announced, his eyes wide with alarm. 'It's got ghosts in it! We better not go any closer!'

'Huh! Mum says there's no such thing. An' anyhow, if any ol' ghosts tried to come after me, I'd punch 'em right in the nose, bang!' Timmy had boasted. But he had been quite willing to run back down the hill to the woods with Boomer.

They hadn't come up here since, because that very afternoon they had discovered a deep cave in a hill down in the very thickest part of the woods. There were all sorts of fascinating things in the cave – part of an old saddle, the remains of a fire covered now with cobwebs, a rusty broken shovel. They had claimed the cave as their very own secret hiding place, and they came to it whenever they could, to sit around and dream up all sorts of things that might have happened in the days of trappers and Indians long ago.

When Timmy had told about seeing the haunted house, his mum and dad had told him that the ghosts were just a make-believe, like Hallowe'en, but they made him promise to stay away from the old farm anyhow. There were pieces of old rusty farm machinery that had stood out in the sun and rain for twenty or more years. A cut from that rusty metal could hurt a lot and be very serious. Also, the Brunsons, who used to live there, were said to have had two wells, and he could easily fall into one of them if he got to running around carelessly.

'Besides,' Uncle Petrie had warned Timmy, 'if the sheriff comes along and catches you trespassin' – which means bein' where you oughtn't to be – it'll cost your folks a fine. There's signs at both ends of Brunson's valley, warning everybody to stay clear. So better keep away.'

So the Brunson homestead, abandoned over twenty years ago, had become a forbidden spot, and Timmy hadn't thought of it for a long time. Now, here he was, with a spyglass he could use to study the old house from a safe distance.

He climbed to the second rail of the old fence, and hooked his leg around the post to steady himself. Then he leaned over so he could get a good look at the whole farmhouse and barn at once. Without Boomer to talk about ghosts flitting around the place, it looked pretty dull and uninteresting.

He took out the spyglass and focused it on the front door of the house. It was boarded up, just as it had been before. He let the spyglass sweep along the front porch, but there was no sign of life there. He turned it towards the barn, idly. But the big doors were padlocked shut.

The rest of the place seemed to be just as deserted as it had been months ago. Timmy put down the spyglass. It was sort of nice to see things bigger through the glass, but when there was nothing special to look at, it didn't seem very exciting.

Lassie saw him start to climb down off the fence, and she barked excitedly, ran over, and picked up the lunch pail by its handle. She couldn't have said it any plainer. She thought it was time for lunch!

'That's a very good idea, Lassie,' Timmy agreed, so they sat down in the shade of the oak tree, and had their lunch.

And when Timmy had eaten all he could hold of the delicious sandwiches and the cookies Mum had packed for him, and Lassie had polished up the bone Mum had put in for her, they both stretched out for a nap.

The last thing that Timmy remembered was the low buzzing sound of the bees that were swarming somewhere in the high branches above him. Now and then one of them would buzz past rather close, but Timmy just let him go. He knew if he hit at the bee and scared it, he might get a painful sting. So long as he let it alone, it wouldn't bother him.

But Lassie didn't really fall asleep the way Timmy did. She just lay quiet, on guard, her nose resting lightly on Timmy's ankle.

And after a little while, she lifted her head suddenly, her long silky ears standing straight up, and listened. Deep down in her throat a little growl started softly. She lay quiet another minute, still listening. Then, slowly, she rose to her feet, stood with her head thrown back, and waited for what would happen next.

It was only a faint noise that the big collie had heard, a far-off sound of metal striking a rock. But it was a man-made sound, and it was enough to put her on guard.

Now she moved slowly to the old fence, rose up on her hind legs, and stood with her forefeet on the rail, looking down towards the old farmhouse. And as she stood there, the growl grew louder in her throat, and the hair on the back of her neck rose threateningly.

A shambling figure was crossing the farmyard, a tin bucket swinging from its hand. It was the figure of an old, bearded man in faded denim suit, and it moved unsteadily towards a rock-rimmed well in the corner of the yard under the maple trees. The well was covered by two heavy planks.

23

The elderly man set his tin bucket down and struggled with one of the planks, pushing and shoving it to get it clear of the well. It seemed to be almost too much for his strength, but he finally managed to dump it to the ground, out of the way.

He rested a moment, leaning on the rim as if to catch his breath. Then he got the tin bucket and carefully let it down into the well on the end of the rope, leaning far over to watch it.

Up on the hill, Lassie barked suddenly down at the man at the well, and Timmy woke with a start of surprise.

The old man, startled by the loud barking, looked up to see where it was coming from, and the rope slipped through his fingers. He made a wild grab for it, missed, and plunged down, heels over head, into the well. His yell of surprise and alarm ended in a big splash.

Up above, Timmy had heard the yell. He staggered to his feet and started over towards the fence. But Lassie wasn't waiting. In a flash, she was through the fence and running at top speed down the hill towards the farmyard.

'Lassie! Come back! We're not allowed to go down there!'

But Lassie kept right on racing down the hill into the forbidden valley as if she hadn't heard Timmy. It was the first time she hadn't come to him when he called her.

Now Timmy heard the call for help again. He couldn't see anyone below, but he knew that Lassie would find whoever it was in trouble. And maybe he had better see if he could help, too.

He climbed through the fence, and a moment later he was running down the hill after Lassie as fast as he could go, calling, 'Wait for me, Lassie! I'm coming, too!'

3

The Stranger

The man down in the well gave a last faint shout as Lassie came coursing down the hill and into the weed-grown farmyard. She stopped midway across it, and threw back her head to sniff inquiringly in all directions.

Then she heard a faint scrambling sound from over at the partly covered old well. She ran to investigate.

She jumped on to the rock-set rim and looked down at the stranger who was hanging on with both hands to a jutting stone, eight or nine feet below. He hung half in the water and half out.

While the big collie watched, the man below reached for a higher rock in the wall, to pull himself clear of the water. But it was wet and slippery, and his hand slid right off it. He fell back into the water with a great splash, and disappeared for a moment. Then he rose sputtering and struggling to reach the rock he had been holding on to at first. When he did catch hold of it, he held on desperately with both hands, panting and gasping.

Lassie barked down sharply at him, and the man looked up hopefully. But when Timmy's round little face appeared suddenly beside Lassie's, the stranger below groaned with disappointment. A small boy and a dog! What could they do? But maybe there was someone else with them!

'Bring somebody to pull me out of here, sonny!' he called up to Timmy. 'Hurry! This water's cold!'

'There's nobody around but me an' Lassie!' Timmy told him. 'But *we'll* help. What'll we do?'

For a moment, the stranger couldn't think of an answer. Then he gasped, 'A rope – there's a long rope – hanging in the barn – right by the side door that's open. Fetch it, and hurry!'

'Right away!' Timmy's face disappeared, and Lassie's with it.

The grey-bearded man, shivering in the icy cold well water, hung on to the wall, but he was getting very tired. His hands were almost too numb to hold on much longer.

The side door that was open was one that Timmy hadn't been able to see from above. He held back in the doorway and stared into the dark interior. He thought suddenly of what Boomer had told him about the place being haunted. He wasn't quite sure he wanted to go in there.

Something nudged him between the shoulders, and he jumped and said, 'Oof!' But when he looked around, it was Lassie. She seemed to be telling him it was all right to go in. And when he still hesitated, she trotted ahead of him, and disappeared into the darkness.

27

'Sure looks spooky!' Timmy told himself, but he went in. He knew Lassie wouldn't lead him any place where it might be dangerous.

It was hard to see anything in there for a moment, but his eyes soon got used to the dimness, and he saw that it was just an ordinary empty old barn. Sure enough, just a few feet away, hanging on a big nail, was a coil of rope.

Timmy hurried over to it, but it was a foot or two higher than he could reach. He would have to climb on to something to get the rope. But on what? There wasn't a bucket or an old sawhorse, or anything that he could stand on. There wasn't even a stick of wood around that he could use to catch a loop of the rope and pull it down.

He tried jumping and trying to grab the loose end of the rope, but it was just too high. 'I guess we can't get it down. We'll have to look for some other rope – or somethin' . . . ' he told Lassie. But he didn't see any other rope, and he decided to try one last jump to grab the rope. He missed by a few inches, lost his balance as he came down, tumbled, and landed sprawling.

Lassie had been standing with her head cocked to one side, watching his antics closely. Now she went over to him and nuzzled him, whimpering.

'I'm okay, Lassie,' he reassured her. 'I was tryin' to pull down that rope,' he pointed to it, 'but I guess it's no use. We'll have to go back an' tell the man.' He began to get to his feet. 'C'mon, Lassie.'

But Lassie ran over to the wall, leaped high in the air, and grabbed the end of the rope.

'You got it!' Timmy shouted happily, and ran to take it from her. The rope came down easily, loop after loop, and in a minute Timmy and Lassie were running out of the barn, trailing it after them.

'We got the rope!' Timmy called down the well. 'What shall I do now?'

'Tie it to the maple tree, and drop me the other end!'

Timmy's knot wasn't very neat, but it held fast as the shivering man climbed slowly with the help of the rope. Halfway up he was so tired that he almost slipped back again. But finally he managed to hook one arm over the well rim, and then it was only a question of a little more effort and he would be safe.

While Timmy and Lassie stood by and watched sympathetically, the elderly man rested a few moments, and then when he had caught his breath, climbed over the well rim and slumped to the ground. He sat with his back against the well, shaking with cold, his eyes closed. Then a giant sneeze startled both Timmy and Lassie.

'Bless you!' Timmy said politely, and Lassie said 'Wroof!'

The bearded man opened his eyes, surprised, and for the first time, a smile lighted up his face. 'Why, thank you! Haven't heard that said for a long time!' Then his face went sober again, and he rubbed his hand across his forehead and muttered, 'At least, not that I recollect.'

'Mum says sittin' around in wet clothes is the best way to catch cold,' Timmy told him solemnly. And Lassie agreed with a small bark.

The man got to his feet. 'Your mum's got good sense. I better get dried off.'

'I guess we'll be goin' now,' Timmy said. 'We're not s'posed to be here, at all. It's tres – trespassin', Dad an' Uncle Petrie said. It's breakin' the law!'

29

The man smiled. 'Well, it's mighty lucky for me you broke the law this time!' He looked very serious and held out his hand to Timmy. 'I'm much obliged, sonny. I dunno if I could've got out of there without your help.'

Timmy grinned happily and took the proffered hand. But when they had shaken hands, Timmy said honestly, 'It wasn't me, really. It was Lassie who heard you, an' she's the one that got the rope for you, too. So you should say thanks to her, 'stead of me.'

The elderly man leaned over and held out his hand to Lassie, quite seriously. 'Thank you, Lassie!'

Lassie gave him her paw and barked softly.

'She says, "You're welcome!"' Timmy explained, beaming with pride. 'Boy! Wait till I tell Mum what she did!'

The man straightened up quickly, his face suddenly darkening. 'You're not to tell her! You mustn't tell *anybody* that you saw me here!'

'But why not?' Timmy was astonished and shocked.

'Because – because' – the man looked about him nervously – 'because they're looking for me. They want to take me back and lock me up again!'

'Back where?' Timmy's eyes were round as saucers. 'Did you run away from some place?'

'That's right, sonny. From a kind of hospital, with a big stone wall around it. They said I had to stay there, but I fooled them. I ran away when the gate was open. And nobody's going to make me go back!'

He looked so stern and angry when he said it, that Timmy felt scared for a moment. But Lassie wagged her tail and went up to the man, nudging his hand with her nose as if she were trying to tell him that she liked him. Or maybe that she felt sorry for him. Timmy decided there wasn't anything to be afraid of, when Lassie acted that way.

The stranger stroked Lassie's head, and seemed to be talking mostly to himself as he went on, 'Seems like I just had to come to this place. I had to find – ' He stopped abruptly and put his hand to his forehead the way he had done before. 'I wish I could think of what I came here for. It was something. I keep trying to remember. But it's no use.' He sighed. 'I'll just keep on trying. I guess it'll come back to me soon.'

'Yes, sir,' Timmy agreed politely. 'I sure hope so.' Then he snapped his fingers to Lassie and told her, 'We gotta go, Lassie. Mum said to get back early.'

Lassie started off at once, eager to be on her way. Timmy had just turned to follow her, when the bearded man called to him. 'Sonny! You won't tell your folks or anybody else that you found me here, will you? Promise?'

Timmy hesitated only a second. Then he said solemnly, 'I promise. Cross my heart.'

'Thanks, boy, I'm depending on you. Now, run along home, or your mum'll start worrying.'

The elderly man in the faded cotton suit watched Timmy and Lassie trudge up the long hill. He seemed to have forgotten that he was cold and wet and that a wind was whipping through his clothing.

When the pair finally reached the top of the hill, Timmy looked back down towards the old farmhouse. The man was still standing looking up at him, and waved when he saw Timmy watching. Timmy waved back, and then climbed through the fence, with Lassie close behind him.

When they had disappeared, the man went slowly

31

into the old barn, and the valley seemed as lonely and empty as if no one had been there for a long, long time.

The sun was almost behind the hills and the woods were full of long shadows as Timmy and Lassie hurried through on the way home. Timmy knew he was already late.

They passed close to the mouth of the big old cave that he and Boomer had discovered last September, but Timmy didn't even slow down. There wasn't time.

He came out about a hundred yards down the creek from the spot where he had lost his fishing pole and reel. He and Lassie had been moving so fast that he was short of breath and had to stop to catch it again. Then he saw something caught between two rocks at the edge of the water. He could hardly believe his eyes! It was his fishing pole, with the new reel still on it!

He ran down the bank to it, with Lassie close at his side. The pole was wedged in between two rocks, but it came out easily when he lifted it from above. And except that his new fishing line was hopelessly tangled around both the reel and the rod, there wasn't anything wrong with it.

But the biggest surprise was still to come! The end of his line was snagged around an old root that stuck up out of the water a few feet away, and there was a ten-inch-long speckled trout caught on his hook! The trout must have grabbed at Timmy's bait the moment it hit the water and, in its struggles to get free, jerked the pole from his hands. The swift current had helped, too, and then had swept both the fishing pole and the trout to the bank.

Timmy grabbed up the fish, which was still wiggling.

'Look, Lassie! We caught a fish! It's a lollypaloosa!' That was one of Uncle Petrie's words, and Timmy liked it because it sounded a lot bigger than ordinary words, even if he didn't know just what it meant.

Lassie took a dainty sniff at the trout, but she kept her distance from the flipping tail. Then she turned and ran up the bank towards the path. When she got to the top, she looked back down and barked sharply a couple of times at Timmy, who was still standing admiring his catch.

'Okay, I'm comin'!' Timmy called to her. 'Quit scoldin'. I know it's gettin' late.' He shouldered the pole, with the trout dangling from the tip of it, and climbed up to follow Lassie homeward.

Mrs Martin was standing in the doorway, watching for him, when he came along the road with Lassie and the trout. Timmy was later than he had promised to be, but she was so relieved to see that he was safe that she let it go without a scolding.

'Look, Mum! Ain't it a whopper?' Timmy dangled the limp trout at her. 'Can we have him for supper?'

'I'm afraid not, dear. Supper's all ready. But when you get your fish scaled and cleaned, we'll put it on ice for tomorrow night's supper,' she smiled. 'It *is* a beauty!'

'C'n I show it to Dad an' Uncle Petrie, first?'

'Of course! They're out in the barn talking to Sheriff Bennett.'

He was starting into the barn, when he heard Uncle Petrie's voice, louder than usual, 'I'm glad you came by to tell us, Carl. We'll be on the lookout.'

'Watch yourselves, though, in case you run into the fellow,' that was Mr Bennett's voice. He was Dad's closest friend. 'That travelling salesman he hitchhiked a

3

ride with from Capitol City is pretty sure he saw the bulge of a gun in his pocket when he got out a mile north of Calverton. '

'What was he in state prison for?' Dad was quite calm, from the sound of his voice.

'Armed robbery. Twenty years to life,' Mr Bennett said. 'They still don't know how he got away.'

Timmy shivered. This was exciting. A real desperate criminal! And he was somewhere around Calverton!

Then he heard Uncle Petrie ask, 'Got a picture of him?'

'Not yet,' Mr Bennett told him, 'but we have a pretty good description of him . . . ' His voice became indistinct as the men seemed to be moving away from the door.

Timmy strained his ears, hardly daring to breathe, but he couldn't hear more than a murmur of voices now.

Lassie nudged him gently with her nose and barked softly. It was long past her suppertime, and she didn't see any use of hanging around here, dangling a dead fish.

But Timmy was thinking about what he had just heard, and slowly but surely he was coming to a frightening conclusion. Could it be – could the escaped criminal be the old man they had helped out of the well in Forbidden Valley?

Maybe he had better go right in and tell Dad all about it. He opened his mouth to call out, and then closed it again abruptly. He had given his solemn promise not to tell anybody about seeing the old man.

'Lassie,' he whispered to the handsome big dog whose eyes were turned up to him with steady affection, 'what shall I do?'

4

Timmy Has A Problem

'If I tell Dad about the man in the well, I'll be breakin'
my promise,' Timmy told Lassie, as he hesitated outside the barn. 'And, anyhow, it couldn't be the same
mean old convict they're talkin' about. *Our* old man was
friendly. You liked him, so he must be all right.'

That's what Timmy told Lassie – and himself. But
he had misgivings. He had never kept this kind of a
secret from Mum and Dad. And, after all, it *could* be
the same man Sheriff Bennett was looking for!

Lassie was getting very tired of waiting around for
him to come to the kitchen and give her some supper.
She barked softly and took him by the sleeve, gently
pulling him away from the barn and towards the house.

'All right, Lassie, I guess you're right,' he told her
soberly. 'We better talk to Mum about it, first, and see
what she thinks.'

But when Timmy and Lassie reached the back step

where Mum had spread out the newspaper for the fish-cleaning, he could hear her talking on the telephone.

He sat down to wait. He was beginning to feel a little dizzy, and his head felt heavy and hot. He could hardly keep his eyes open as he leaned back against the porch post and listened drowsily to Mum's voice.

Timmy looked at the very dead trout that had to be cleaned. Somehow, he didn't feel like it. 'Wish you hadn't grabbed that worm,' he said disgustedly. 'Hey, Lassie, do you want this?' he asked hopefully. But Lassie sniffed disdainfully at it and turned away with a sharp little whine.

Ruth came out to the porch. She saw Timmy's spotted face and heavy eyes and bent over him quickly, feeling his forehead. It was burning with fever.

'Mum, there's somethin' I've got to tell you,' Timmy said drowsily. 'It's about the haunted house, an' – '

'Never mind it now, dear. It's too bad to spoil your birthday celebration, but you're headed for bed, right now!'

'But Mum, it's important!'

'It can keep. Off we go, Mister Measles!' She led him inside, her arm around him to steady him.

Timmy was glad to lean against her, and to let her help him undress and get into bed. He felt awfully tired, and he wanted to sleep. But just before he drifted off, he opened his eyes and a frown puckered his forehead. 'Mum, there was somethin' I wanted to ask you, but I just can't seem to remember it now.'

'Don't worry, dear. It'll come back to you. Just go to sleep now.'

'All right, Mum.'

Ruth Martin bent and kissed the hot little forehead.

36

'Good night, dear.' But Timmy was too drowsy to do more than mumble, 'Night, Mum,' before he was fast asleep.

Ruth was closing the door after her when she glanced back into the room and saw that Lassie had slipped in unnoticed and was now sitting beside the foot of Timmy's bed, her chin resting on the covers.

'Come on, Lassie!' Ruth whispered. 'Come get your supper!' But for once, the magic word 'supper' failed. Lassie only blinked at her and didn't move. Ruth had to go in again and lead her out.

Ruth closed the door softly and patted Lassie's head. 'Sorry, girl!' she whispered. 'I know you hate to leave him, but he'll be all right. It's just measles, and he'll be up and around in a little while.'

The house was very still at midnight. The moonlight was streaming in through Timmy's window, as he sat up in bed staring blankly about the room. 'We got to find the rope,' he said worriedly, 'or the poor old man will drown!' He pushed back the covers and swung his feet to the floor.

A moment later, he was staggering across the room towards the door. Ruth had left it open so that she or Paul could hear if Timmy called out during the night. She had already been in twice to check on him, and found him fast asleep and still flushed with fever. Timmy moved silently on his bare feet along the hallway towards the kitchen.

But Lassie was there, on guard, lying as close to the closed kitchen door as she could get, and she heard him at once. She rose when the door started to open, and moved aside, watching curiously in the dark as Timmy groped his way dizzily towards the rear door.

When he didn't speak to her, she knew that something was the matter. She moved suddenly between him and the door. Timmy bumped into her, and tried to push her aside, muttering feverishly, 'Go 'way, Lassie. I have to look for the rope!'

Lassie held her ground, though Timmy tried to walk around her to reach the door. Then she barked softly, protestingly. She couldn't seem to understand what was wrong with him.

For a moment, when Paul heard her bark, he thought she might be warning them against an intruder. The escaped convict came quickly to his mind. He leaped out of bed and ran down the hallway towards the kitchen, not even stopping to find a weapon. Ruth was right behind.

A quick glance into Timmy's empty bedroom told the story, and they hurried to the kitchen as Lassie barked again. Timmy stood blinking as the light snapped on, and they could see by the dazed look in his heavy-lidded eyes that he had been sleepwalking in the grip of the fever.

Paul caught Timmy up in his arms. 'Back to bed, young fellow!' he told him, and Timmy sighed and snuggled down with his head on Paul's shoulder.

But a few minutes later, when Paul and Ruth had him safely back in his bed and tucked in, Timmy lifted his head sleepily and peered at them. 'Don't send him back, please, Dad. He's such a nice ol' man. An' Lassie likes him, too.'

'Don't worry, dear. Everything will be all right!' Ruth laid a cool hand on Timmy's burning forehead. He sighed and sank back on the pillow, smiling.

They left Lassie stretched out in front of his closed door.

'What old man was he talking about? I wonder,' Paul frowned. 'Do you suppose there's any chance he's met – ' he broke off abruptly, but a moment later he shook his head, smiling. 'I guess not. If he'd met that runaway convict, he'd hardly call him a nice old man. Bennett says Sanders is a very tough character.'

'He tried to tell me something about the Brunson farm,' Ruth said, 'but I didn't pay much attention.' She looked worried. 'It's farfetched, I realise, but I wonder if you ought to tell Mr Bennett. That deserted farm *would* be a good place for someone to hide out. No one ever goes there.'

'I'll think about it. I have to go into town tomorrow morning anyhow, and I may drop in to see Carl.'

Dr Wilson came by in the morning, though he didn't have to look at Timmy to know that he had caught the same fever as his pal Boomer. 'Just keep him quiet for a few days,' he told Ruth Martin. 'And tell Lassie to stop looking so miserable. Everywhere I turn around here, I see her staring at me. She's worse than an old mother hen about that youngster!'

Paul had driven into town to get some spare parts for the plough and to look at a good secondhand tractor that he was thinking of buying. It would take most of their savings, but the tractor was badly needed, and he and Ruth had decided to do without a new stove for another year or two, to get it.

He found Carl Bennett in his office, studying the bulletin from the state prison, with Blackie Sanders's picture and record.

'Whew! He's a mean-looking character, judging by

39

that picture of him!' Paul commented.

'Probably flatters him, at that! Run your eye down that record.'

Paul glanced at the list of Sanders's crimes. 'I always suspected I didn't want to be a policeman,' he said with a grim smile. 'Now I'm sure of it!'

Carl Bennett sighed and dropped the bulletin into his desk drawer. 'The worst part of it is not knowing where to look for him. There hasn't been even a rumour of anybody seeing him since that travelling salesman came in with *his* story. I'm hoping he kept right on hitch-hiking to the ocean – *either* ocean!'

'Don't tell me you couldn't use the reward!' Paul grinned.

Carl squinted at him, and tapped the badge he wore pinned to his suspenders. 'Line of duty. No reward money. But it might get me re-elected next fall – if I could find him and bring him in.' Then he added, half to himself, 'And didn't get shot full of holes doing it!' He chuckled, but his eyes were unsmiling.

'I might have a lead,' Paul said, growing serious abruptly. And he told the sheriff about Timmy's mention of the old man and his reference to the Brunson farm.

'It probably doesn't mean a thing,' Paul concluded, 'but Ruth and I both thought you might like to take a look around the Brunson place, to be on the safe side.'

Carl got up without answering, and went over to the map on the wall opposite his desk. With his finger, he traced the main highway from Capitol City, the road on which the salesman had picked up the hitchhiker. There were many small unimproved roads leading off from the highway as it neared the hills. As he studied the map, he nodded slowly. 'The more I think of it, the likelier it gets that Sanders might be right there. I think I'll take a look this morning.'

He took a service revolver from his desk drawer and checked it to see if it was loaded. Then he dropped it into his side pocket and reached for his hat. 'Thanks, Paul. Even if it turns out to be a false alarm, I'm glad to be out doing something besides sitting here and waiting for word that he's used that gun on somebody.'

Paul nodded understandingly. 'I'd like to go along, if you say so.'

'Sorry,' Carl told him soberly, 'I don't have an extra gun to lend you. And you can't take a chance with a killer like Sanders.'

Paul smiled. 'I thought of that. So I brought along my rifle. It's in the back of my car, under some sacks. I got it out of the house without Ruth seeing it.'

Bennett hesitated. Then he laid his hand heavily on Paul's shoulder for a moment, and said gruffly, 'All right. Come on, but don't let me catch you trying to be a hero!'

They found the gate at the end of Brunson's little valley still firmly chained shut. Grass was growing high all about the gate and as far as they could see from one end of the valley to the other. It was lush and lovely after the spring rain, but there was nowhere a sign that a human foot had touched it.

'Better leave the car here, and not break the gate lock,' Bennett said. 'Walking's good, and it won't give him warning that we're coming – if he's here.'

'Sure looks deserted!' Paul stood off when they had come up to within a hundred yards of the house and barn.

41

'First time I've had a close look in years,' the sheriff admitted. 'The old place certainly stands up against the weather. It's been empty twenty years.'

'What happened to the Brunsons?' Paul asked, as they stood under a lone maple and watched for a sign of life at either the boarded-up house or the barn.

'Brunson's wife died of an operation, suddenlike. Left a boy of ten. Brunson couldn't stand it here without her, and just picked up one day and took the boy to the city. Place has been shut up ever since.'

'It's a shame,' Paul shook his head. 'I'd say, just at a glance, this is some of the best land in Calverton County.' There was a wistful tone in Paul's voice. 'Things ought to grow like wildfire here.'

'Guess they did,' Bennett admitted, 'and it's a shame somebody can't take it over and make a good living.'

'Who's handling the property?' Paul asked.

'A bank pays the taxes every year, out of a fund that Brunson left there. Some city bank on the East Coast.' Bennett saw the hungry look in his friend's eye, and went on, with a twinkle, 'And there's no use trying to lease it. That's been tried. The bank says "No deal."'

'And Brunson probably living in Paris or some such place while it lies idle!' Paul scowled.

'Well, it's his, and if that's what he wants to do with it, it's his business!' Bennett grinned. 'Let's move up and take a good look around. I don't think there's anybody within a mile or two, but we might as well be dead sure.'

They were alert for danger as they came up to the house. But they could see that the windows and door were heavily boarded, and there was no sign of anyone having broken in.

42

Carl Bennett, scanning the recently dried ground between the well and the house, stopped suddenly, pointing.

The tracks of a man's heavy shoes were all around. They had unmistakably been made since the rainstorm of the night before last. They led back and forth between the barn and the half-covered well.

Carl took out his revolver, and Paul balanced his rifle, ready for a quick shot, as they followed the tracks towards the barn and around to the side door.

The small side door was open a few inches, and moving gently in the spring breeze. The two men exchanged knowing looks. The man they were hunting was either inside here, or gone.

Tense, ready, Carl Bennett motioned his friend to stand out of the line of fire, as he went up to the small door. Paul obeyed, but kept his rifle levelled towards the doorway.

Inside the old barn, high up in the darkness of the almost empty hayloft, the grey-bearded man was watching the narrow slit of light that was the doorway.

He had been waiting for this moment ever since he had seen the red-painted car stop outside the gate.

5

Who Was It?

The grey-bearded man in the hayloft held his breath as he stared down towards the slowly opening side door of the old barn. He lay half-hidden in the musty old hay, and wisps of it clung to his hair and beard.

The loft ladder lay beside him, and he hoped desperately that its absence would convince the men who were coming to look for him, that it had been gone as long as the barn had stood empty.

Now as he watched the door, he saw it swing wide. Then, in a flash, the square-shouldered figure of a man blotted out the sunlight. He could see that the man had a revolver in his hand.

Terrified, he looked around the loft for something he could use as a weapon. But there was nothing. Not even a chunk of wood. And it was too late for him to try to run.

The sunlight was streaming through the empty doorway again. That meant that the big man with the gun was inside.

The man in the loft shivered and put his face down in the hay. The dust from it nearly made him sneeze, but he managed to stop it in time. He could hear the men below whispering, over near the door, but he couldn't make out what they were saying.

A spot of light played on the ceiling of the hayloft and danced about searchingly for a moment. Then it was gone. It had missed the hidden man by only a few inches.

'No sign of him now, but somebody's been here, all right.' The voice had the snap of authority.

'Yes, I saw the ashes of a little fire out in back. He probably warmed up some food on it,' the second man agreed. And he added, 'The poor devil!'

The first man's voice had a sharp edge to it. 'Save your sympathy for the people he's robbed and killed, Paul. Sanders is no better than a wild animal, judging by the list of crimes he's committed.'

Their voices died away as they went to the door and out.

The grey-bearded man sat up and stared after them. 'Sanders,' he repeated dazedly. 'My name's Sanders. And I'm a killer. I didn't know.' He buried his face in his hands and sat huddled there a long time.

He didn't even lift his head to look over towards the small side door as it was slammed shut. The sound of a hammer nailing a board into place echoed through the empty barn.

After a while he lifted his head, and there was a look of bewilderment on his face. 'It won't come back to me, nohow. Lord help me, I can't remember. Even the name don't seem like it belongs to me. "Joey," they called me at the hospital. Not "Sanders". Never "Sanders" that I recollect. And if I ever killed anybody, it's gone from my mind ...'

Suddenly he looked frightened. 'I guess maybe I better go away from here and hide someplace else. They might come back again and catch me sometime when I'm sleeping. And they'd lock me up again.'

'We missed him by a couple of hours, I'd say. The ashes of his fire were still a bit warm,' Carl Bennett said, as they drove back towards Calverton.

'Looks like Timmy did see him there, after all,' Paul looked serious. 'If the youngster wasn't running a high fever, I'd ask him some questions. Sanders may have dropped a word about where he was going, some such thing.'

'Not much chance of that. Sanders is too smart.'

'Seems funny,' Paul looked thoughtful, 'Timmy saying he was a nice old man. And Lassie apparently taking to him, too. It certainly doesn't fit the description of Sanders that the state prison's sending out!'

Carl Bennett laughed suddenly. 'Y'know, I've been thinking that myself. How do we know that was Sanders? Maybe it was some old tramp that broke into the Brunson place to get out of the rain and hung around a couple of days resting his feet.'

Paul grinned back at him. 'Well, we had a nice ride on a pretty spring day. So there's no harm done, either way!'

But a few days later, when Timmy's fever had finally disappeared, Ruth Martin came into the kitchen from Timmy's room with his breakfast tray, and told her husband, 'Better go talk to Timmy, dear. He wants to tell you something.'

Paul looked stern. 'And I want to tell *him* something about breaking his promise not to go near that farm!'

Ruth smiled. 'That's what is on his mind. He feels pretty bad about it. It seems some old man fell into the well there, and Lassie went to his rescue. Timmy went after her before he'd stopped to remember his promise.'

'Does he suspect his "nice old man" may have been that escaped convict, Sanders?' Paul asked grimly.

'I'm afraid he *did*!' Ruth admitted, 'but I told him that Carl and you decided it was probably some harmless tramp, and he seemed a lot relieved.'

'Relieved?'

'It seems he promised not to tell anyone he had seen the old man. There was something about being afraid of having to go back to some *hospital*.'

'Timmy and his promises!' He shook his head and started towards the bedroom. 'I'll talk to him about that.'

'Paul!' Ruth looked serious, and when Paul turned with a look of inquiry, she said softly, 'Don't forget he's only nine.'

'Don't worry, honey!' Paul smiled.

She knew Timmy would say he was sorry he had broken his promise, and Paul would bring in the fishing rod, with a whole spool of brand-new line to take the place of the tangled one. And they would have a grand time planning their summer fishing trip, everything else forgotten.

And that's what did happen. And Timmy was allowed up for supper, for the first time in several long days.

47

The next morning started an exciting day for the whole Martin household. Paul and Uncle Petrie were up at dawn getting ready to go to Calverton and pick up the newly bought tractor and drive it home.

Timmy, up and dressed as early as they were, and even more excited, hoped they would take him along. But Ruth explained gently to him that as long as he had those few little pink spots left on his face, he was better off not going into town. There wasn't any danger now of his giving the measles to other children, but not all the mothers understood that, and Ruth didn't wish to worry them.

'Mum!' Timmy had come charging in from the yard, with Lassie bounding at his heels. 'What'll I do?'

'Well, there's that jigsaw puzzle Boomer's mother sent you. And you haven't looked at that book about horses that your teacher brought by.'

Timmy's lower lip stuck out. Ruth could see that her suggestions weren't getting over. 'Aw, I'm tired of puzzles an' books.'

'Why don't you and Lassie go on a hike? Maybe Boomer would like to go with you. I'll fix you a nice lunch. Peanut butter and jelly sandwiches and a banana for each of you. What do you say?'

Timmy's eyes sparkled. He had a lot of things to tell his chum. 'Can I call him right now?'

Ruth laughed. 'I'm afraid he isn't even awake yet. The sun is barely up, you know. But I'll fix the lunch anyhow, because I'm sure he'll want to go.'

Timmy's mother had guessed right. Not only did Boomer want to go on a hike, but his mother was glad to bring him over in the family car and leave him.

The two mothers watched their sturdy youngsters

48

start off down the road, fishing poles over their shoulders and Lassie cavorting ahead of them.

'I'm glad we don't have to worry about the Brunson farmhouse any more,' Mrs Bates said, over a cup of coffee.

'Why, what's happened there?' Ruth was surprised.

'Now, don't say Miss Jenny hasn't told you that the Brunson boy has come back and is moving into the old place!'

Ruth shook her head. 'I guess she thought we were such newcomers to Calverton that we wouldn't be interested.'

'Young Brunson was only a kid about Boomer and Timmy's age when his pa took him away, after the mother passed on.'

'Does he have a family?'

'I don't know. All I heard is that he got the keys from Attorney Blake last week, and said he'd move in soon. Blake says he wasn't even too sure how to find his way to the valley, but he said No when Blake offered to show him. Guess he seemed like a feller with a load on his mind and set on keeping it to himself.'

'Well, as you said, we won't have to worry about the boys climbing on that old rusty machinery any longer or falling into the well,' Ruth said thankfully.

Timmy and Boomer hadn't quite made up their minds in which direction to hike. They stopped to talk it over before they reached the woods.

'I'll show you where I caught that whoppin' big trout,' Timmy boasted. 'Maybe I'll catch another one like it.'

'Aw!' Boomer frowned. 'I don't feel like fishin'. I'd rather look at the haunted house through your spyglass.'

'We'd have to go through the woods!' Timmy didn't

mind changing his plans. 'We can stop at our cave an' eat our lunch!'

'Let's climb the hill *first*, an' then come back to the cave when the sun's shinin' towards it. It ain't so spooky in the sunshine.' Boomer was an inch taller than Timmy, and it made him want to be the one who did all the planning. Which was generally all right with Timmy, who didn't care who made the plans just so long as he was in on them.

They left their fishing poles hidden in thick brush beside the creek, and started the long hike up the slope of Old Blue Top. Lassie ran ahead as usual.

And as they went, Timmy told Boomer all about his and Lassie's adventure with the old tramp who had fallen into Brunson's well. 'But when Dad an' Mr Bennett went out to look for him, he was gone!' Timmy concluded.

Boomer scowled. 'I bet you made it all up,' he said finally. 'You're fibbin'.'

Timmy stopped and faced him. 'No! I'm not!'

'Ah, pooh!' Boomer didn't want to believe Timmy was telling the truth. Nothing so exciting had ever happened to *him*.

'I'll show you the well he fell into! Then you'll have to believe me!'

'I'm not allowed to go there! An' neither are you!'

'I mean from up on top of the hill. With the spyglass.'

'Huh! A lot you could see from there!' Boomer was beginning to be convinced. 'A well's a well!'

Timmy knew he would have to add a clincher. He looked mysterious and even whispered, though there was no one within a mile but Lassie and themselves,

'Mr Bennett and Dad think maybe he was the 'scaped convict from the state prison!'

Boomer's eyes fairly popped out. 'Gee!' he breathed. 'The one they never did catch? The – the killer?'

Timmy could see he was almost convinced now. He nodded vigorously and added, 'An' I coulda captured him if I'd had a gun!'

'Wow!' Boomer swallowed that without a bit of doubt. He stared at his pal with new respect. 'Weren't you scared?'

'Uh-uh!' Timmy shook his head. 'Lassie was along.'

That made sense to Boomer, and they trudged on up the hill side by side, more than ever anxious to take a good look at the Brunson farmhouse. There was always a chance that the mysterious stranger would be down there again!

But when they had reached the top of the hill, and climbed to the top rail of the old fence, they didn't need the telescope to see that something new was going on down at the farmhouse.

6

The Brunsons

The front door of the farmhouse was wide open now, and the heavy boards had been removed from the windows. A sedan was standing in front of the porch and a trailer piled high with furniture was hitched to it. Even from Timmy's distance on the hill, he could see that it was an old sedan, even older than his family's.

'Somebody's movin' in!' Timmy excitedly adjusted the telescope. Now he could see a little girl about his and Boomer's age, sitting in the sedan with someone who was probably her mother. A tall man in shirt sleeves was carrying a couple of cane-bottomed kitchen chairs into the house.

'There's a girl, but I don't see any guys,' Timmy frowned. He handed the telescope to Boomer with a disappointed sigh. 'I guess that's all there is! A girl!'

Boomer adjusted the telescope and stared through it. 'Hey!' he exclaimed, 'she's gettin' out of the car, an'' she's carryin' something! It looks like a – a *cat*!'

Timmy could see the white fluffy object that the little girl had set on the ground. It moved on wobbly legs. But it was certainly not a cat. It was a white puppy.

'That's a puppy!' Timmy said. 'It's called a poodle. I saw one in town a long time ago.'

'It's a cat!' Boomer insisted. 'I know a cat when I see it!'

As Lassie whimpered at the object below, Boomer got a bright idea. 'Scat, Lassie! Go get him!'

In a flash, Lassie was bounding down the hill.

Timmy jumped up, yelling, 'Lassie! Come back here!' but the big collie paid no attention to the call. 'Now look what you've done!' Timmy wailed to Boomer. 'She'll scare the puppy!' And then he, too, slipped through the railing and started galloping down the long hill with Boomer close on his heels, both yelling to Lassie to come back.

The woman in the car heard the yelling, and looked up. She saw a big, shaggy dog rushing down the side of the hill, followed by two boys who were yelling something. She gave a frightened scream and jumped out of the car to run to the little girl.

'Letty!' She reached the startled litle girl and caught her up in her arms, holding her tightly and staring terrified at the big collie that had almost reached the foot of the hill. 'Dave! Help!' The mother was hysterical, and the little girl started to cry loudly.

The puppy had seen Lassie coming and was running to meet her now, its tiny tail wagging happily. But Dave Brunson, rushing out of the house to see what was wrong, saw only what seemed to be the attack of a vicious dog.

He looked around desperately for a weapon he could use to beat off the strange animal, but all he could find was a wooden slat that he had pulled off one of the furniture crates. With that in his hand, he ran towards the attacker.

Lassie slid to a stop. She sniffed at the small white object as it came up and in puppy fashion lay down and rolled over on its back, legs waving in the air. It was saying, as appealingly as it could, 'Please don't hurt me, Big Dog. I'm just a helpless pup and I want to make friends.'

Lassie's tail started swinging. But Dave Brunson didn't notice it. He saw the puppy rolling on the ground and he thought Lassie had hurt it.

Letty was screaming, 'My puppy! Don't let the bad dog hurt my puppy!' and at the same time struggling to get out of her mother's arms and run to her puppy's rescue.

Timmy reached the yard a couple of seconds after Lassie and the puppy met. He saw the man running at his collie with a stick, and he ran between, yelling, 'Don't hit Lassie!'

Brunson brushed him aside and kept going, but Timmy got to Lassie first, and threw himself to the ground beside her, arms around her neck. 'No! Don't!' he shrieked.

But the stick was already coming down, and Brunson couldn't stop it in time. Instead of hitting Lassie, it struck Timmy a glancing blow on the shoulder, and Timmy cried out in pain.

In a flash, Lassie had leaped at Brunson and grabbed his wrist in her teeth, snarling and growling. Brunson staggered back, trying to shake her off. 'Let go!' he yelled, dropping the slat.

But Lassie's teeth were clamped on the wrist of the man who had hurt her young master, and it wasn't till Timmy hollered at her to let go, that she dropped away from Brunson. She backed off, showing her teeth in a snarl and keeping between him and Timmy.

Timmy put his arm over her neck, and held her, glaring up at the man. Boomer had stayed a safe distance, and was watching, scared. 'You hit me!' Timmy accused.

Dave Brunson looked worried. 'I didn't mean to hit you, sonny. I was aiming at that dog of yours. I thought he was about to chew up our pup.'

'Lassie isn't a he. She's a she. And she never hurt a puppy or anybody else!' He kept his arm protectively around Lassie.

'Dave! Send them away!' Mrs Brunson called sharply. She still clung tightly to Letty, but the little girl was struggling to get free.

'Let me down, Mamma!' she pleaded. 'I want to pet the big dog!'

'No, no!' Her mother held on to her even more tightly. And then, hysterically, 'Dave! Don't just stand there! Chase that awful dog away! Get him out of here!'

'We're goin' right now!' Timmy said defiantly. And as the small white puppy cavorted around Lassie, trying to tempt her to play, he said, 'Go 'way, pup!' And he started towards the hill, pulling Lassie along. 'Come on, Lassie!'

Boomer fell in behind, and followed across the yard.

And the puppy came right along after them.

Dave Brunson watched them start up the hill, and sighed. He was sorry he had struck the small boy, even though it had been an accident. He made up his mind he would find out who the child was, and make a point of apologising to his parents as soon as possible. Probably someone in Calverton would know who the two boys were.

'I hope you told them never to come on our property again,' Meta Brunson told her husband shakily.

'I don't think they will, dear. I think the big dog was just being friendly with Pom-Pom,' he soothed her.

She had let Letty down, once the boys were out of the farmyard. Now Letty was off like a flash, after them.

'Letty!' she called. 'Come back here!' But Letty was already starting up the hill after the two boys and the dogs. She plunged into the heavy brush at the base of the hill, paying no attention to the brambles that tore at her dress.

'Pom-Pom! Here, Pom-Pom!' she shouted.

Timmy and Boomer stopped and looked back, startled. They hadn't even noticed that the poodle puppy was following them and Lassie. It was only a few feet behind them, and having difficulty climbing on its very young legs.

'Shoo! Go back!' Timmy waved an arm at Pom-Pom, but the pup kept on coming. And when it reached the place where Lassie was waiting with the boys, it danced up to her and started leaping at the patient collie's ear, trying with puppy impudence to catch and worry the fascinating turned-over tip. Lassie took the assault good-naturedly, but when the sharp little teeth nipped her ear, she growled a little and shook her head.

The puppy danced back to take another nip, and Lassie decided she had had enough. She lifted one paw and put it firmly down on the wiggling pest. The puppy yipped a protest and tried to wriggle free, but Lassie held it down in spite of its whimpering struggles. She knew she would be due for more ear-chewing the moment she let the puppy up.

Timmy and Boomer were both laughing heartily at the scene, when Letty came struggling up the hill. She misunderstood. It looked to her as if the big collie intended to make a meal of her puppy. 'Pom-Pom!' she wailed, and began to cry loudly.

Lassie lifted her foot, and the puppy rolled free and bounced over to greet Letty. She was surprised and delighted, and snatched it up in her arms. Pom-Pom promptly made a frantic attempt to lick her face, its small body one big delighted wiggle.

'Lassie wasn't hurtin' the puppy,' Timmy reassured Letty solemnly, and she gave him a shy smile.

There was a shrill call from the farmyard. 'Letty! Come back here this instant!'

'Yes, Mummy!' Letty called down, and started away with the puppy in her arms. But she hadn't gone more than a couple of steps when she turned and faced the two boys. She smiled sweetly at Timmy, and announced, 'My name's Letty, boy. What's yours?'

Timmy looked startled. Then he said hastily, 'Timmy Martin.'

'Good-bye, Timmy. I'll see you again!' And then she giggled, turned, and fled down the hill with Pom-Pom yapping in her arms.

'Girls!' said Boomer disgustedly. 'They're all silly!'

'Lassie's a girl, an' she isn't silly!' Timmy reminded him.

'That's different,' Boomer admitted seriously. 'Lassie's – well – Lassie's a dog girl, an' it isn't the same as being a people girl.'

Timmy wrinkled his forehead. 'I guess not. Anyhow, let's have our lunch, an' then we can go to the cave.'

So they trudged on up to the brow of the hill where they had left their lunch pail and the telescope, and were soon enjoying the tasty sandwiches and cookies and milk that Mum Martin had packed for them. Lassie came in for a full share of the food, as usual.

Timmy's shoulder felt sore, and he pulled off his shirt to look at the shoulder that the man had hit with the wooden slat. There was only a small bruised spot to be seen.

Boomer eyed it sympathetically. 'I bet your pa'll get the police after that feller.'

Timmy looked shocked. 'The police?'

'Sure! They'll throw him in jail – quick! Bang!'

'But he didn't mean to hit *me*! He was after Lassie 'cause he thought she was going to bite Pom-Pom!' Timmy insisted. And he added soberly, 'It wasn't his fault I got in the way.'

'Just the same –' Boomer liked to argue.

Timmy interrupted, with a wide grin, 'Anyhow we're even! Lassie bit his wrist. An' I bet it hurts more'n my shoulder!'

Dave Brunson's wrist did hurt. Lassie's teeth had clamped down hard when she made him drop the slat, but she hadn't broken the skin.

'That awful dog!' Meta Brunson said angrily. 'If

those boys and that dog ever come here again, I'm going to take a broom to all three of them!'

Her husband sighed. 'That's hardly the way to get along with the neighbours. You forget we're not living in the city any longer. This is our home, and there's no sense getting off on the wrong foot with people we'll have to be friends with.'

Meta frowned and looked around her at the dust that lay inch deep on everything. It would take hard work to make it into any sort of a home, she thought. And she didn't know if she wanted to make friends here.

'We should have sold this place,' she said bitterly.

Dave looked at her, and his shoulders dropped dejectedly. 'I tried. You know that. But the only offer we had was so low I had to turn it down.'

'I still can't see why we have to *live* here!'

'Because we own it. And because it's going to do Letty a world of good to live in the country!' Dave Brunson's voice was firmer now.

'But you've never done any farming!' Meta was repeating an old argument. 'You don't even know how to start!'

'There are plenty of men in Calverton who'll be glad to give me the right advice!' Dave put his arm around his wife's waist. 'We'll make it somehow, honey!'

7

The Cave

When Timmy and Boomer came down off the hill and started home through the woods, the sun was still high overhead. They stopped beside the creek where their fishing poles were hidden under the bushes.

'Let's fish awhile,' Boomer suggested. 'We got lots of time.'

'You can fish if you want to,' Timmy told him, 'but I want to see if anybody's been in our cave an' took my rock collection while we've been havin' the measles.'

'Guess I'll go, too,' Boomer agreed. His legs were aching from all the climbing uphill and downhill, but he couldn't let Timmy think he was tired.

They trudged along, pushing through tall brush that seemed to have grown enormously in all directions since their last visit before the big storm. Lassie was, as usual, trotting ahead, alert for danger, stopping every now and then to sniff the air and look about her sharply.

The tall trees, with their masses of new leaves, met and interlaced overhead, making a sort of green umbrella that almost shut out the warm spring sun. The few shafts of sunlight that filtered down through the leaves were tinged with a pale green. The woods seemed filled with the colour.

Boomer looked at Timmy and laughed. 'You oughta see your face! It's green!'

'Huh!' Timmy grinned back, 'no greener'n yours, I bet!'

So they headed for home. The cave would be there another day. They had plenty of time. There wasn't much chance of anybody else finding it, with the brush so high.

But somebody *had* found it! At that very moment, a little wisp of smoke was curling out of the mouth of the cave and losing itself in the clear air. And if anyone had been close enough to get a whiff of that smoke, they would have smelled the aroma of broiling fish!

Deep in the old hiding place, the grey-haired man who called himself Joey was leaning over a small wood fire and watching a small trout sizzling on the end of a green twig. It was a primitive way to cook, but it was better than eating raw fish.

Joey had broken out of the Brunson barn five days ago, as soon as Carl Bennett and Paul had driven away in the red car. He had retrieved his small food supply and water can from where he had hidden them in the old hayloft when he had seen the two men drive up to the farm gate.

Then he had climbed to the top of Old Blue and plunged down its other slope into the woods. And for two days, he had hidden there, without seeing anyone, but always fearful that the law would catch up with him.

Finally, his food used up, Joey had made a twilight visit to Calverton. He had slipped into a small grocery on the far edge of town to spend his last dollar for lard, beans, and flour. He had waited till the grocer was alone.

Sam Moss had spent twenty-five years behind the counter of his small grocery and notions store. He had waited on the tall, bearded man with hardly a second look. He had been anxious to close up and get home so that he could take his shoes off, and hoboes of all kinds were no novelty in Calverton. They drifted through every springtime, as soon as the weather turned warm. And he saw nothing about this old fellow that looked different from his fellow tramps.

So Joey had disappeared back into the woods with his small stock of food. It was only after Sam had gotten comfortable in his old easy chair on the home porch, that he had wondered if he hadn't heard something last week about Sheriff Bennett looking for a bearded escaped convict.

'Shucks!' He settled down with his paper. 'No chance of this feller being him. He had a sad look, but he certainly didn't look like a killer!'

The next morning Joey had stumbled on to the secret cave as he pushed deeper into the woods.

The cave made an ideal place to hide, warm and dry. There was even a small cotton blanket which someone had left there not too long ago, and a pile of firewood. The blanket kept off the night cold, and by day he used the old dusty firewood for his cooking. From somewhere deep in his memory, he recognised that he was lucky to have found the old wood. It would burn with much less smoke than newly gathered kindling, and that was important to a man who was in hiding. The less smoke, the smaller chance that anyone would see it and find him.

He had made several friends during his short stay. A doe and her fawn had come sniffing around the mouth of the cave.

Now the fawn and its mother came early each morning, the first of a string of visitors. There was a family of woodchucks who lived in holes nearby, and popped out to stare at him, wiggling their tiny ears. A great many birds came there, too.

Joey tried to see that they all had something to eat, but his supply of flour was beginning to get low. And he had no money to buy more. 'We got to go slow, boys,' he told the woodchuck family, but he wasn't too much worried. He was beginning to feel almost safe here.

It was only now and then that he had bad moments, thinking back to the things the man with the badge had said about him. Then he would try desperately to bring back the memory of his past, but he never could.

That night, Timmy was quieter than his parents were used to. Usually, he bubbled over with stories about things he had seen and done on his hike. Instead, he didn't seem to want to talk about it at all. He just picked at his supper and pushed his dessert away untouched.

Ruth and Paul exchanged worried looks. Then Paul asked lightly, 'What's on your mind, skipper?'

'Nothin' much!' Timmy squirmed uneasily.

Ruth leaned over and felt his forehead. 'I shouldn't

have let you and Boomer take that long hike today. It was too soon.'

'Do I have the measles back?' Timmy seemed to brighten at the thought.

'No, dear,' Ruth smiled, 'you're all over them. But you're going straight to bed after supper, and no radio programmes for you tonight.'

Uncle Petrie looked over at Timmy's sober face and gave an amused snort. 'I do believe he misses all the babying!' He was only teasing to make Timmy smile, but it didn't work. Timmy just sat looking down at the table.

Paul laughed. 'Not Timmy! He's not a baby, are you, son?'

Timmy looked at him without a smile and sighed. 'No, sir.'

'Well, then, man to man, what's bothering you?' Paul looked serious now.

Timmy sighed again. 'I guess I better tell you, only Boomer said – ' he broke off wrinkling his forehead in a worried frown.

'What did Boomer say, dear?' Ruth asked gently.

'He said you'd get the police after the man. An' it wasn't really his fault, honest! He didn't mean to hit me!' Timmy poured it out without taking a breath.

'Timmy! Who hit you? What's all this about?' Paul demanded sternly.

Timmy gulped and hesitated. Ruth laid her hand quickly over his on the table. 'Go on, dear. We'll understand.'

'Out with it!' Paul frowned. This might be serious.

'Well – it's about me an' Lassie. We tres . . . ' – he had a little difficulty with the word – 'we trespassed. An' the man thought – ' A knock at the door interrupted him.

A stranger stood in the doorway. At least, he was a stranger to the three older people. But Timmy knew him. It was the man from the haunted house. The very one he had just been starting to tell them about!

He had a coat on now, and his hair was neatly combed, but there was no mistaking he was the same man. Lassie recognised him, too, and she got up from where she had been lying beside Timmy's chair, and started stalking towards the door, her head lowered, and a deep growl in her throat.

Uncle Petrie caught her by the collar and held her back. 'Whoa, there, girl! That's no way to say hello!'

'I'm afraid I don't blame her!' The stranger smiled faintly. 'I'm David Brunson.' He seemed to think that would explain Lassie's growl.

Uncle Petrie and the Martins looked puzzled, but Paul rose and went to the door with his hand outstretched. 'Glad to know you. We heard that you and your family were moving back into the old family place.'

Dave Brunson took Paul's hand in a hearty handshake, but now it was his turn to look puzzled. 'Didn't the youngster tell you what happened there today?'

Paul looked startled. 'At your place? Why, no!'

Timmy's voice interrupted. It was a very small voice. 'I was just beginnin' to.'

Paul frowned. What was it Timmy had started to tell them about a man striking him?

Dave Brunson saw the frown. 'The whole thing was a misunderstanding. I thought the dog was vicious, and I was trying to drive it off.'

Ruth had come over to them. 'I believe that's what Timmy was telling us when you knocked. Why don't you come in and have a cup of coffee with us, and we'll find out what our son was doing on your property, after promising to keep off it?'

8

Getting Acquainted

'I'm glad you came by.' Paul Martin was walking to the Brunson car with Dave.

Dave had told the Martins what had happened that afternoon, and had been relieved to find that they realised that he hadn't meant to strike Timmy. Timmy had promised that he and Lassie wouldn't 'trespass' again. He would wait to be invited.

'We'll be settled in a few days, and then we'd like you folks to come and have coffee with *us*,' Dave had told Ruth as he left.

'Indeed, we'll be glad to come!' Ruth had assured him.

But now, as he and Paul crossed the farmyard to the old car, Dave Brunson spoke frankly.

'My wife has lived in the city all of her life. It may take her a while to get used to country life, especially the – ' he hesitated, hoping Paul wouldn't take offence, 'the social life. I remember, when we lived here, Mother always had the house full of Ladies' Aiders and her Sewing Circle. But Meta's never had time to make many friends, with our delicate little girl on her hands.'

'I'll tell Ruth to slip a little hint to the Calverton ladies to take it slow. But I think Mrs Brunson will like them when she gets to know them.'

'I think so, myself,' Dave smiled. 'I know Mother managed to be happy, even though there wasn't much money around. What Dad couldn't afford, we did without. And never missed it, while Dad and I had her.' He looked sad, suddenly, remembering.

'She passed away before you left Calverton, didn't she?' Paul didn't intend to pry, but he sensed that Dave Brunson wanted to talk.

Dave nodded. 'That's why we went. Dad couldn't stand the place without her. It was like – like he was only half alive after she'd gone. He boarded up the place and we went to live in the city.'

'You must have missed the valley,' Paul said quietly.

'I did, for a while. But I was only ten, and life in the city was pretty exciting for a kid. That is, till Dad went into the army after Pearl Harbor, and didn't come back.' He gave a twisted grin. 'I bounced around for quite a few years, but I never thought much about the old house until the doctors told us Letty needed to get out of the city. Then we –' he hesitated a moment, and then corrected himself, '*I* decided to try to make a go of the farm, and see at the same time if it would help Letty get strong.'

Paul laughed. 'It will! All you have to do is look at Timmy and our little neighbour, Boomer, for proof of what fresh milk and home grown vegetables can do!'

'I hope you're right!' Dave sighed. 'I'm gambling all I've got on it!'

Paul Martin watched his visitor's old sedan disappear down the road into the darkness, coughing and rattling in the rutted dirt. As he turned to go back into the house, he was thinking, 'From the looks of that old car, they haven't much to gamble with!'

Later, he talked it over with Ruth, and she agreed that it would be better to let the Brunsons get settled before anyone went calling. She meant to be quite firm about it with Boomer's mother, Mrs Bates, who was already making plans to drop in and welcome the new-comers right away.

It was only a few days later that Timmy came dashing into the Martin kitchen, where his mother was ironing. 'Mum! Mum! I just saw Mr Brunson! An' he says he's bought a pony for Letty!' The screen door slammed as Lassie followed him in.

'A pony!' Ruth felt a little twinge. That was one of the things she and Paul had talked about getting for Timmy this spring, but they had had to postpone it because of the new tractor. 'Why, that's fine!'

'He says Letty's going to learn to ride! An' I can come see the pony!' He was breathless with excitement. 'Can we go today? Me an' Lassie?'

'It seems a little soon, dear! Better wait till Letty's had a chance to get acquainted with the pony herself.'

Timmy looked disappointed for a moment. Then he brightened again. 'Well, can I go tell Boomer about it?'

'Of course! But be back early!'

'Yes, Mum!' And a moment later, the door slammed after him and Lassie.

Timmy found his pal Boomer out in the Bates barn,

busily hammering together a somewhat rickety chicken coop for the baby chickens his folks had promised him.

Soon, he dropped the hammer and said, 'It's too hot to hammer. Let's go wadin'.'

Lassie barked and sat up, waving her paws at Timmy. 'Hey! She wants us to go!' Timmy interrupted. And Lassie started leaping around as if she understood what they were saying.

'Okay,' Boomer agreed. 'But we better take some sandwiches. I'll tell Mum.'

But Mrs Bates had driven into Calverton to attend a meeting of the Sewing Sisters of her church, so the boys had to make their own sandwiches. And the sandwiches that they made and wrapped in yesterday's newspaper were somewhat different from Mrs Bates's usual peanut butter and jelly concoctions. They were sky-scrapers!

By the time Boomer had put together a slice of last night's roast beef, some cold bacon, some jelly, and an inch thick gob of peanut butter topped with pickle slices, the top piece of bread was three inches from the bottom one!

And Timmy had to have the same mixture in his sandwich.

So they were well equipped for the expedition as they set out with Lassie for the woods.

But when they got to the edge of the creek and Boomer stuck a timid toe into the water, it was a lot colder than they had expected. He said, 'Ow!' and pulled his toe out in a hurry. 'It's too cold!'

Even Lassie, after daintily taking a drink at the water's edge, backed away and shook herself. Timmy could see that she agreed with Boomer!

70

'What'll we do instead?' he asked. 'I'm not hungry yet.'

'Let's go to the cave!' Boomer suggested. 'It's cooler. An' we can be hunters hidin' from Indians.'

'Swell!' Timmy agreed.

So Boomer put on his shoes again and they set out through the woods. Lassie trotted ahead, while the boys made believe that there were hostile Indians tracking them to get their scalps.

But the only thing that got in their way today was the thick brush and its thorns that snatched at their clothes. And in a little while they had pushed through the worst of it and were almost in sight of the cave.

Lassie ran ahead and went out of sight.

'She knows where we're going!' Timmy grinned, and began to hurry.

But when they came up to the big clump of rocks that were their final landmark, they heard Lassie barking excitedly.

Timmy, knowing Lassie's barks, said, 'It sounds like she's glad to see somebody. That's her "Hello" bark!'

'Maybe somebody's found our cave!' Boomer scowled.

'An' my rock collection!' Timmy looked worried.

Boomer wasted no time. 'Come on! We'll just tell whoever it is that we found the cave first, an' they got to go!'

They hurried on, spurred by Lassie's strangely friendly barks. It was most likely some of the kids from the Calverton school. They both hoped they weren't big ones!

When they came in sight of the cave, all they could see at first was Lassie's rear end as she faced somebody

71

inside. It looked as if it had turned out to be an old friend, because Lassie's tail was waving a mile a minute. But for a moment, because of the darkness of the cave, they couldn't make out who the friend was.

'Lassie!' Timmy's voice was a little sharp. There was a teeny bit of jealousy in it.

Then a man stepped out into the sunlight, and Timmy recognised him. 'Hi!' he greeted the grey-bearded man. And he told Boomer excitedly, 'It's him! The man who fell in the well at the Brunson farm!' And he ran forward, with Boomer close on his heels, to shake hands.

Joey was glad to see Timmy again, and his eyes brightened at sight of what Timmy called 'only our lunch' in the newspaper-wrapped packages. He was sick and tired of fish, and getting so low on beans and flour that he had to dole both out sparingly. Even his friendly little animal pets had been on short rations the last couple of days.

Timmy was happy about being able to show the man to Boomer, because Boomer never had believed Timmy and Lassie had really helped anybody out of the Brunson well. Now Timmy had the living proof of it.

'That's right!' the grey-haired man told Boomer. 'I'd a'been down there yet, if Timmy hadn't come along with this smart dog of his!'

That having been settled, Boomer discovered he was getting hungry. So he sat down and unwrapped his sandwich, and began to eat it without noticing the old man's hungry looks.

But Timmy had gone inside to check on his rock collection, and he had noticed the almost empty flour sack and the scant half cup of beans on the wooden shelf. And when he came out again, he saw Joey's eyes.

72

Timmy unwrapped his own sandwich, and then pushed it aside. 'I guess I don't feel hungry,' he told Boomer. 'An' you always cut the bread too thick.'

'It's how I like it!' Boomer mumbled through an over-stuffed mouth. 'Give it to Lassie if you don't want it!'

'She doesn't like pickles, an' peanut butter sticks to her teeth,' Timmy explained. Then he shook his head sadly, 'But it sure is a shame it has to go to waste!'

'If you're real sure you don't want it . . .' Joey's voice trailed off.

'Golly, would you eat it for me?' Timmy made believe he hadn't even thought of that before. 'Mum says it's wrong to throw away good food, so if you'd eat it for me, I'd be much obliged!'

'Thanks, sonny. Guess I can manage it!' Joey took the sandwich slowly, and even held back from biting into it right away. But Timmy could see by the size of the bite he took when he did start to eat, that he was good and hungry.

Boomer had eaten half his sandwich when he decided he'd had plenty. He lifted his arm to toss the remains into the bushes, but Timmy stopped him by calling out, 'Don't be a litterbug! Don't be a litterbug!' in the singsong of the first grader.

Boomer stopped midway in his throw. 'I wasn't going to do it,' he scowled. 'I was just pretendin'.'

Old Joey suddenly said, 'Sh-h-h!' and put a finger to his lips. They both looked startled and a bit scared. Joey's eyes twinkled, and he pointed over at the brambly thicket. 'Look there!' he whispered.

They both stared, but for a moment they couldn't see anything in the bushes. At Timmy's elbow, Lassie lifted her head and stared, too. But she didn't growl, and the tip of her tail wagged gently.

Now they could see something moving, and make out the outlines of two deer, a doe and her fawn. Then two brown heads were thrust through the bushes, to stare back at the group out of great soft brown eyes.

'Watch, and hold real still!' Joey whispered. Then he slowly tossed a piece of Boomer's bread to the deer. It fell on the ground in front of the doe.

For a moment the doe ignored the bread, staring suspiciously at the two boys and the dog. Then, swiftly, she pushed out of the bushes, snatched up the bread in her teeth, and in a moment had backed out of sight again. A second later, the fawn's head disappeared, too, and then the boys heard them both crashing off through the brush and scampering away.

Both boys were delighted. 'Will they be back?' Timmy asked excitedly.

'Throw some more bread and they'll come back!' Boomer ordered, but Joey looked over at Lassie, who was sitting up straight now, staring after the deer and making little worried noises in her throat. 'I doubt it, son. I'm afraid they won't come around again while Lassie's here. They don't know she wouldn't hurt them.' He picked up the remainder of Boomer's sandwich, and wrapped it in the newspaper again. 'I'll save the rest of this bread for them to eat tomorrow.'

'Let's go home,' Boomer suggested. Now that the show seemed to be over, and he had had enough to eat, he was getting bored with Timmy's friend.

'Okay,' Timmy agreed, and scrambled to his feet. 'They were cute. I hope we can see them again.'

'I've got some other folks around here maybe you'd

like to get acquainted with, too. Some of them are so friendly, they'll come right up and eat out of your hand!' Joey smiled at his two young visitors.

'We'll sure be back!' Timmy assured him. 'Real soon!'

'Meantime,' the grey-haired man said soberly, 'I'd take it as a favour if you boys wouldn't tell anybody you saw me here.'

Boomer frowned. 'How long you gonna use our cave?'

'Just a few days, son,' Joey assured him, 'then I'll be drifting on. I'm just resting here.'

'I guess it's okay, then,' Boomer conceded, ignoring Timmy's frown, 'if we get it back soon.'

'You can stay as long as you like!' Timmy told the grey-bearded man firmly. And then with a defiant look at his pal Boomer, 'An' we won't say anything about it because me an' Boomer have got a solemn pledge not to tell *any*body *any*thing that happens in our cave.' He waited for Boomer to admit it, but Boomer just looked sulky and kicked at the ground. Timmy persisted, 'Haven't we?'

Boomer squirmed and scowled, but he finally got out a 'Yeah'. But he still wasn't too happy about somebody else enjoying their special cave. He glanced up at the sun and told Timmy abruptly, 'We gotta hurry. It's gettin' late.' He started to turn away, then remembered his manners. 'Good-bye, Mister — say, what's your *name*?'

'Joey,' the old man said softly. 'That's it. Joey.'

'Just Joey?' Boomer looked startled. 'What's your other name, the one people write on your letters?'

'Got no other one. Don't really need it, seeing I don't

75

get any letters,' Joey told him soberly. 'Joey's enough.'

Boomer eyed him sharply. It didn't sound right to him.

'Aw! C'mon! You were in such a hurry! Let's go!' Timmy couldn't see the point of wanting to know Joey's last name. 'Joey' was a nice easy name to remember.

So Boomer and Timmy started off for home, with Lassie trotting ahead.

Joey watched them go out of sight among the trees, and shook his head grimly. 'I sure wouldn't want those nice little fellers to know I'm hiding from the law!'

9

The Helping Hand

They were hardly out of sight of the cave before Boomer said, 'Let's hurry! We got to tell Mr Bennett where he's hiding!'

'But we can't! We promised!' Timmy was shocked.

'But you said your pa thought he was the 'scaped convict! Maybe we can get a reward for capturing him!' Boomer reminded him.

Timmy held back. His face was a little red as he confessed. 'I guess I fibbed. He *isn't* the convict. I know.'

'Yah!' Boomer scowled at him. '*How* do you know?' He looked suspicious. 'You're just making it up.'

'If I tell you, will you promise not to tell anybody, cross your heart?' Timmy whispered mysteriously, though the only possible hearer was Lassie, waiting impatiently for them to start walking again.

'Uh-huh!' Boomer agreed, hastily making the required gesture. 'Go ahead.'

77

So Timmy told him about the old man having run away from some hospital. 'An' he has to hide, or they'll drag him back an' lock him up. An' he hates it.'

'Is that all?' Boomer was disappointed. He had expected something a lot more exciting, maybe spies and stolen maps, like the picture stories in the comic books.

'That's plenty!' Timmy assured him stoutly. 'I guess he had to take shots, an' stay in his room. I guess you'd run away, too.'

'Yeah,' Boomer nodded thoughtfully. 'Maybe it *would* be mean to let them find him.'

So they trudged on home, chattering and trying to guess what kind of wild animals old Joey would have to show them when they went back to the cave next time.

But old Joey wasn't thinking of his wild pets just then. He was still very hungry, as he took the newspaper wrappings off the sandwich Timmy had given him. There was a lot of the thick sandwich left, enough for two or three good bites now, and plenty for the morning.

Then, as he started to eat, his eyes wandered to the headlines in the paper he had tossed aside. All of a sudden his appetite was gone.

He stared at the words that seemed to jump out at him. CONVICT STILL AT LARGE, the top line in the *Calverton Tribune* read, and below it, SEARCH GOES ON IN WIDE AREA FOR DESPERATE CRIMINAL.

He put aside the sandwich and picked up the paper with a hand that shook. 'No trace of the dangerous Blackie Sanders has been found since he was reported in the vicinity of our town nearly two weeks ago,' he read. 'Sheriff Bennett promises to keep a sharp lookout for the escaped convict though he is of the opinion that the man Sanders has escaped into one of our neighbouring states by this time and is in hiding there.'

Joey sighed with relief as he laid the paper down. He was safe so long as he could stay hidden.

He didn't think the boys would tell about seeing him. But if it did slip out, and a search party came, Joey felt that he was familiar enough with the woods now, to slip away from the cave in time and hide in one of the many thickly overgrown hollows he had discovered.

Timmy woke up even before Lassie had made her customary visit to his bedroom to pull off his covers and roust him out of bed. He sat up in bed and tried to think what it was he wanted to do today. Something had made him wake up early, but what?

Then he remembered. He and Boomer were going out to the cave to see old Joey.

But as he sat up in bed, planning, he suddenly realised that there was no sunshine pouring in through the window.

It was raining. The kind that kept on, and on, till everything was muddy. Sometimes it lasted for days.

There was no telling how long it would keep up now. One thing was certain, though. He and Boomer wouldn't get back to the cave today. Or maybe not for a couple of days.

He flopped back on his pillow and pulled up the covers. No use now getting up early.

Ruth Martin was being quieter than usual as she moved around the kitchen, getting breakfast for Paul and Uncle Petrie, who were out in the barn doing the chores.

Lassie was lying close to the hall door, with her

head between her paws. She was pretending that she was dozing, waiting for word to go wake up Timmy, but when Ruth pulled out the chairs at the table and spread the chequered cloth, Lassie lifted up her head and looked eagerly for Ruth to say, 'Go wake Timmy!'

'Not yet,' Ruth told her softly. 'We'll let him sleep awhile this morning.'

Lassie gave a long sigh and settled down again.

'Sometimes,' Ruth told the intelligent big collie, 'I think you can understand just about everything we say.'

'And some of the things that we just *think*!' Paul chuckled. He had pulled off his muddy boots on the back steps, and was in his socks, carrying his dripping raincoat and hat. 'I hope she doesn't read my mind right now! I'm thinking some mean things about this weather coming right when I had the south field ready to sow!'

Uncle Petrie was coming in as Paul spoke. He hung up his wet slicker and hat, and padded over to the sink to wash up beside his nephew. 'They tell me the old-timers counted on their rheumatics to warn them about sloppy weather. Some folks still claim it works.'

'I'll depend on the bureau!' Paul grinned. 'That's one service we farmers would be glad to pay for!'

'That reminds me.' Ruth brought the coffee over as the men finished washing up and sat down in their places. 'The Brunsons haven't ordered a phone yet.'

'Can't figure anybody not wanting a phone. 'Specially with a sick young'un in the house,' Uncle Petrie frowned.

Paul looked thoughtful. 'Might be the expense.

Stringing a wire out to their valley would cost them considerable.'

'It'd be worth it. Then Brunson could get the weather by phone, till the electric company got around to running a power line to his place,' Uncle Petrie insisted.

'I've got a feeling the Brunsons aren't too well fixed,' Paul said, frowning.

'What makes you think that?' Ruth was surprised.

'That ancient car he drives. And I hear he's using that old plough of his father's that's been standing out in the open for twenty years. And hiring a horse to pull it!'

'No tractor?' Ruth was shocked.

Uncle Petrie and Paul both laughed at her expression.

'There's a lot of places left in the world where they haven't heard of tractors!' Uncle Petrie grinned at her.

'But everyone in Calverton uses them. And I think it's a shame if the Brunsons can't afford one, and nobody offers to lend them one!' Ruth flashed at the two men.

Paul and Uncle Petrie stopped grinning suddenly, and Paul told her soberly, 'You're right as usual, Ruth. And as soon as the rain stops, I'm going to take a ride over to Brunson's and see how they're making out.'

'We won't be needin' the tractor, after we get the south field seeded. Maybe you could lend it to them,' Uncle Petrie suggested.

'I had that in mind,' Paul agreed.

A sudden heavy downpour almost drowned his words, and they looked apprehensively towards the windows.

'Wow! A lot of planting's gonna be washed out today!' Uncle Petrie predicted.

*

Dave Brunson stood on the edge of the field that he had ploughed and seeded just yesterday, with back-breaking labour. It was a sea of mud in all directions. The carefully mounded earth around the seeds of his hybrid corn had been flattened out by the downpour. Even the furrows had been almost destroyed by the crosscurrent that had swept down off the hill at the height of the storm.

He had all his labours to do over again.

It was a dismal prospect. But worst of all was the thought of having to tell Meta of the disaster. They had counted on the cornfield. Their crop was to pay for some of the comforts they had to do without now – a stove that wasn't falling apart, a new pump in the kitchen sink.

Instead, he would have to get more seed, rent the plough horse again, and go through all the hard work once more. Maybe only to see another storm wash away the new planting!

He started back along the muddy road towards the farmhouse, and hardly heard the car that had come up behind him. A voice called out, 'Brunson!' and he turned, startled.

It was Paul Martin at the wheel, and his wife and Timmy were in the rear seat with Lassie between them.

'Hope you don't mind people dropping in!' Paul called. 'I want to talk to you, and the whole family wished themselves along!'

'Why – ' Dave's hesitation was very slight. He wasn't sure how Meta would take the unexpected visit. She wasn't used to the easy informality of the country. 'Why, of course! My wife will be happy to see you folks. I've been telling her what pleasant neighbours we have.'

Timmy leaned forward hastily. 'Lassie won't scare the puppy. I warned her to be real gentle.'

'I'm sure you did!' Dave laughed.

He climbed into the front seat of the sedan, and rode with them into the yard.

Meta Brunson glanced out of the window and saw the car pull in. She drew back in dismay. For a moment she thought of running to the bedroom and locking herself in. She hated to meet strangers in an old faded house dress.

The kitchen was clean. Even the old stove was polished and shining. But everything in the room seemed to have poverty written all over it.

She whipped off her apron, smoothed her hair, and ran to the living-room. The few sticks of furniture seemed lost in the big old room, but there was a cheerful fire on the hearth, and the curtains she had just hung up today – made of old sheets and dyed a pretty pale pink – were fresh and perky.

She could hear the voices of her visitors as they came towards the porch, and she steeled herself to smile her warmest when she greeted them. She opened the door, smiling.

But when she saw Timmy and the big collie bringing up the rear of the procession, she lost her smile.

Ruth was quick to notice that Meta wasn't pleased to see the big dog that had frightened her. She told Timmy, 'Timmy boy, there's no sense in your bringing Lassie into the house. Why don't you take her for a little walk, and then wait in the car?'

'But I want to see Letty! An' Lassie wants to see Pom-Pom!' Timmy protested.

'Letty's in the barn with her pony,' Dave Brunson

told him quickly, 'and Pom-Pom's sure to be there, too.'

'Mum, why can't we go see them?' Timmy coaxed.

Ruth looked at Meta and waited for her to speak. Meta hesitated a moment, then she nodded reluctantly.

'All right,' Ruth told him sternly, 'but don't forget your manners! And don't play too rough. Remember, Letty's only a little girl, not as strong as Boomer is!'

'Okay, Mum! We'll remember!' And he and Lassie tried to outrun each other to the barn.

10

The Quarrel

Dave Brunson and Paul had left the two mothers to get acquainted over a cup of tea, while they took a stroll around the property. Paul didn't hesitate to tell Dave Brunson how much he envied him the fine piece of land. 'Once you get the hang of farming,' he told Dave, 'you should make a good living here. It's the best soil in the township.'

'Do you really think so?' Dave asked eagerly.

Paul took a handful of the damp dirt, and crumbled it between his fingers. 'Rich! You should have bumper crops.'

Dave made a grim face. 'I suppose anybody with a little know-how would! But I'm just a greenhorn. I can't even keep the seed in the ground! Look at that field! It's one big mud puddle!'

'You can't blame yourself for the weather!' Paul smiled at his neighbour. 'That puddle ought to be dried off in a couple of days, and the ground will be just right for working!'

'I'd better start arranging to get that horse again, and a new supply of seed!' Dave looked glum.

'Tell you what!' Paul pretended the thought had just occurred to him, 'Why don't you use our tractor? It would get the work done in half the time!'

'I'm sorry – I can't afford to rent it. I'm – a bit short of ready cash,' Dave said honestly.

'Who said anything about renting?' Paul grinned. 'We still have one field to plough and sow. After that, the big gas eater will be just standing around till harvest. You might as well use it!'

Dave's eyes lighted up. Then he shook his head slowly. 'Thanks, but I don't believe in borrowing.'

Paul was silent a moment. Then he put his hand on Dave Brunson's shoulder and said, 'I'm sorry you feel that way, Dave. Around here, we don't consider it a disgrace for a man to borrow his neighbour's tools, so long as he takes good care of them. And if a man is too proud to borrow them, we naturally have to judge that *he* wouldn't lend his own tools to someone who needed them.'

'If I had anything worth lending you in return,' Dave answered, 'it would be different! But the way it looks now, I'm licked before I start!'

'Dave!' It was Meta's voice, and as Dave turned in surprise at the happy tone of it, he saw her and Ruth hurrying towards them from the house. Meta's face was radiant. She looked happier than he had seen her since they had come here. 'Wait till you hear what we've been planning!'

'When we go over to get the tractor,' Meta told her

husband gaily, 'Mrs Martin is going to lend us a round maple table that matches our kitchen chairs. It'll just fit in the kitchen by the window!'

Dave looked startled. Paul caught his eye and grinned.

'The boys can tie it on the back of your car,' Ruth told her, laughing. 'And they'd better tie it on tight, or it'll fall off and get smashed into kindling when Dave comes along behind you in the tractor!'

'I'll strangle him if that happens!' Meta giggled. 'You saw how much furniture we have!'

Dave looked at Paul and Paul looked at him, and Dave made a gesture of resignation. It seemed that the ladies had settled the borrowing question! All he could do now was to go along with it.

'I'll send Timmy over on his bike as soon as we get the seed in,' Paul promised. 'Should be in a couple of days.'

On the way home, Paul teased Ruth about getting so well acquainted with Meta Brunson at their first meeting. 'How did you do it?' he grinned. 'Dave told me she didn't make friends easily, and was here sort of against her wishes just for Letty's health.'

'Oh, I don't know. I liked her right away. And I've always believed that if you like someone, really like them, they're bound to feel it, and they can't help being friendly. I'm sure we'll get along fine, all of us.'

The next day, Uncle Petrie and Paul ploughed the south field. The new tractor performed like a champion, and the work was finished in just a few hours. Then there was only the sowing of the seed to do, and that wouldn't take long, either.

Timmy and Lassie watched for a while, and Timmy had a couple of rides on the tractor, with Lassie running alongside and keeping up a steady barking. It was great fun for both of them, but Paul finally got tired of the noise and shooed them away.

Timmy sauntered back to the yard, and he and Lassie sat outside the barn. Spring vacation was nice, for a day or so, but it got pretty boring after that. School wasn't so bad, after all. There was always something interesting going on.

There was a lot of stir and bustle inside the house today. Mum was engaged in a mysterious something called spring cleaning. It meant that all the furniture had to be moved, and the curtains taken down. And the vacuum cleaner was going for hours. And after it was all done, it didn't look any different to Timmy and the other two male members of the household, than before it all started. But it seemed to be something that happened at everybody's house, and it had to be endured.

The telephone was ringing. Mum's voice answered it and a couple of minutes later, she called him.

'Boomer's mum has started her spring cleaning, too. How would you like to take Lassie and meet Boomer at the creek? She's packed him a lunch, and I can fix one for you, too.'

Timmy's eyes brightened. Maybe if they started right away, they would have time to go to the cave and see the old man again! 'Golly, Mum! That would be swell. But – don't bother about fixin' my lunch. I can do it myself.'

'That's a good idea! I'll just keep on with my work. Take whatever looks good to you!' Ruth told him.

It took only a few minutes for Timmy to fill his lunchbox, but when he got through, it was just about the heaviest lunch box in history. And the cold roast in the icebox looked like a skeleton of its former plump self. In addition to the lunch box full of sandwiches and cake, Timmy stowed a couple of apples in his pockets and a handful of last night's biscuits inside his shirt. His friend at the cave was going to have plenty of crumbs for the birds and the deer.

Boomer was under their special tree beside the creek when Timmy and Lassie got there. He had his fishing line in the water, and was leaning against the tree with his hands clasped behind his head and his eyes closed.

Timmy was panting. That heavy lunch box and his fishing pole weighed more than he had counted on.

He threw himself down on the soft grass beside Boomer. 'Whew!' He rubbed a sleeve over his perspiring face. 'Thought I'd never get here!'

Boomer opened his eyes and yawned. His fishing cork was still bobbing idly on top of the water. He looked at Timmy and frowned. 'What'cha got inside your shirt?'

'Biscuits for the deer, an' the other wild animals at the cave,' Timmy boasted, and pulled one out to display it. 'I got apples, too. And meat and stuff. I bet Joey'll be glad to see us.'

'Yeah, if he hasn't got scared an' run off!'

Timmy looked worried. 'But he said he'd stay a few days! And we promised to come back. He wouldn't just leave, without telling us.'

'He would, too,' Boomer looked scornful. 'He's only a tramp, no matter what he told you! An' my pa says tramps are no good. They steal an' –'

'Not Joey! An' he's not a tramp! He's a nice ol' man, an' I betcha he's still in the cave! An' I'm goin' to see! You can stay here if you want to!'

'He is too! He is too!' Boomer yelled.

11

The Forgotten Fish Pole

Timmy and Boomer tramped through the woods towards the old cave, carrying the lunch boxes and their fishing poles.

'You don't have to come if you don't want to,' Timmy reminded his friend.

'I know it!' Boomer scowled. 'An' I wouldn't go, just to see that ol' tramp. But I want to see the animals.'

Timmy nodded happily. He was glad to have Boomer along on any terms. Weren't they best friends?

Long before they came in sight of the cave, old Joey knew he was going to have company.

Joey had slipped into the cave and just inside, in the shadows, he waited tensely for the first sound that might let him know who the visitors were. But suddenly he relaxed. The two young voices that he was hearing were the voices of his two little friends who had promised to come back and see him. He wondered if they had remembered to bring some crumbs for the birds.

He sat down outside the cave and waited for them. In a moment, Lassie bounded up, with the boys a few yards behind her. She sat down beside old Joey, put a paw on his lap, and offered her silky ear to be scratched.

Boomer was friendlier today. 'Where's the wild animals?' he asked.

Joey looked startled. 'The wild – *animals*?'

Timmy threw a reproving look at Boomer, and then explained politely, 'He means he'd like to see some of your pets you told us you'd show us.'

'Oh!' Joey grinned. His momentary distress had vanished.

Pink clouds were floating across the sky above the trees. That meant that the sun must be pretty low. Timmy scrambled to his feet. 'I guess we oughta get on home,' he suggested.

So in a few minutes, they were on their way back to the creek, and it wasn't till they were halfway home that Boomer noticed that Timmy had left his fishing pole behind at the cave.

Timmy had forgotten all about it. 'Golly! We better go back and get it,' he told Boomer.

'It'd be dark before we got home,' Boomer objected. 'My pa would spank me.'

'Well *I'm* goin'! I'll run all the way,' Timmy announced boldly, 'an' I bet I get home before dark.'

'Go ahead,' Boomer told him coldly. 'But I bet you don't get *this* far before it gets dark! Well – so long!' He turned away and tramped out of sight with his own fishing pole safely over his shoulder.

Timmy stood with his hand on Lassie's ruff, looking

after his friend. Then he looked back towards the darkening woods out of which they had just come. 'Come on, Lassie. We'll hurry both ways,' he told her, a little shakily.

But Lassie stood where she was and made no move to go along with her small boss. He took a few steps, and then looked back. 'You comin', Lassie?' he demanded.

Lassie barked sharply, but stayed where she was. Quite obviously, she had no intention of going back to the cave. And from the tone of her bark, she didn't approve of his going, either.

'Aw, Lassie! I *got* to get my fish pole!' he pleaded. But the shadows were heavy now in the direction of the cave, and somewhere up out of sight in the green branches, an owl had started to hoot mournfully. 'Hoo-hoo,' it called, 'hoo-hoo!' It was just plain spooky.

For a moment more, Timmy hesitated. Lassie stood firm. Then Timmy came back slowly to her. 'Okay, Lassie. We'll go home. But I sure think Mum is going to be awful mad when she finds out I left my pole an' my new reel someplace.'

Lassie nudged his hand with her nose. 'Hurry up,' she seemed to be saying, 'and don't change your mind again!'

So they kept on, and got home safely before Mum had had time to worry. But Timmy, washing up for supper, whispered to Lassie, 'I kinda wish you hadn't made me come home. I still think I could have got there an' back by dark.'

But it was a good thing that he hadn't gone back to the cave. Because old Joey had another visitor now, a most unwelcome one.

12

The Unwelcome Guest

The two boys and Lassie had hardly disappeared in the woods, when old Joey saw his friend the doe come through the brush, with her fawn close beside her.

He coaxed them over with a handful of the new grass that was growing close to the mouth of the cave. It was a pretty sight to see them moving gracefully about, without fear. He wished that the boys could still have been there to watch.

But after only a few minutes of browsing, the mother deer suddenly lifted her head, sniffed suspiciously, and then bounded away in long, graceful leaps. And the fawn ran off close on her heels.

Now he heard what had alarmed them. It was the sound of someone coming through the brush. For a moment, he thought that it might be the boys, coming back for the rod and reel that Timmy had left standing against the rocks beside the cave entrance.

But he decided quickly that it was someone or something else, because the sound was coming from the opposite direction.

It might be the law, catching up with him at last!

Joey snatched up the fishing pole and tossed it inside the cave. Then he hastily picked up what was left of the picnic lunch, and started into the cave with it.

He wasn't quite out of sight when a man's gruff voice called out, 'Hey, you there. Where d'ya think you're goin'?' and then, 'Get your hands up!'

Joey turned slowly, the remnants of the food dropping from his hands as he raised them. But it was no shiny-badged law officer who stood watching him. It was a tall, gaunt man in ragged cotton clothes and wearing a thick beard and shaggy, uncut hair. His small black eyes were set close together under heavy brows, and there was the look of a hunted animal in them. He had a long-nosed revolver in his right hand. And it was levelled at Joey.

As Joey stared, his hands still at shoulder height, the big man strode forward, his eyes fixed on Joey suspiciously. But the old man was so obviously frightened that the intruder decided he was harmless. He came up to him, turned him around, and felt quickly for a revolver in Joey's pockets. Not finding one, he stuck his own gun into his belt and told Joey, carelessly, 'You can put down the mitts, gran'pa! I ain't aiming to hurt ya, long as you do like I say!'

Joey lowered his hands slowly, but his eyes still mirrored his fear. 'Y-yes, sir,' he stammered.

The big man demanded suddenly, 'Anybody staying here besides you?' He was looking around suspiciously. 'Where'd them sandwiches and all that meat come from? And biscuits!'

Joey explained hurriedly, 'Coupla little boys come by. That was their lunch. But they're gone now.'

'Good thing I didn't run into them.' The dark man looked mean. 'I don't like gabby kids.'

'They won't be back. Maybe not for days,' Joey said quickly. 'Days and days. Maybe not at all!'

'That's fine! I figure to take myself a little rest for a few days. I been travelling considerable, lately.' The man gave a short, harsh laugh.

'Cave's pretty damp, mister.' Joey wanted to discourage his unwelcome guest.

'I can stand it, I reckon. It's bound to beat sleeping out in the open!' He saw through Joey's attempt to discourage him, and a crooked grin made his cruel mouth look even meaner. 'So save your breath, old-timer! You got company, like it or not! And don't try to sneak off and hunt up the law!'

'Never had such an idea,' Joey told him quietly. 'The law's no friend of mine.'

The black-bearded man studied him. 'Yeah. Well, don't get any notions about trying to square your own self by turning me in.'

'Not likely,' old Joey shook his head wearily, 'even if you didn't have that gun.'

The big man seemed convinced. 'Now, s'pose you stir around and see what kinda supper you can scare up? I'm almighty hungry.'

And when Joey had managed to put together a sort of a meal, of odds and ends of the lunch and a couple of biscuits that he had made with the last of his flour, the big man ate hungrily and wanted more.

'Got nothing more,' Joey told him. 'Maybe tomorrow I can catch a fish or two, though.'

'Fish?' The black-haired man scowled. 'That don't tickle my fancy none. A rabbit's more to my taste. You got a trap in that cave we could use?'

Joey caught his breath. A trap for his friendly little animals! 'A what?' he asked, looking blank. He was stalling for time, hoping desperately to think of some way to keep the stranger from rigging up a snare.

'A *trap*, old-timer! Something to catch a meal in!' The big man looked disgustedly at Joey's stupidity.

'Oh, a trap!' Joey looked vague. 'Nope. None in there when I came, and I got no money to buy one, even if I could take a chance on being seen in town to do it!'

The bearded man shrugged. 'Then I guess it's fish tomorrow. But we'll figure some way to get us some good red meat after that!'

Long after the intruder was snoring in the recesses of the deep cave, old Joey squatted by the embers of his fire. He could gather up his small possessions and sneak off during the night. That would rid him of the unwelcome guest. But if he did, where would he go to hide?

He hoped that the big man would get tired of the cave in a day or so, and would go on his way. But most of all he hoped that the two boys and Lassie wouldn't come back till the stranger was gone.

Towards dawn, he took Timmy's fish pole and went to the brook that wound its way through the heavy brush and down into the big creek. Before the first rays of the sun had lightened the sky, he had two plump yellow perch that should make a tasty breakfast for his visitor.

As he made his way back to the cave, Joey hurried his

steps. He heard the black-bearded man stirring inside the cave, yawning loudly.

'Long as I aim to stick around awhile,' he told Joey after breakfast, 'we might as well get acquainted. What do I call you?'

Old Joey hesitated. If he told the stranger that he was the escaped convict Blackie Sanders, there was a good chance that the visitor would turn him in to the police for the reward. So he told him, 'Just Joey.'

'Joey, hey?' The black-haired man laughed. 'Okay, pop. Joey it is! And you can call me Blondy!'

'Blondy?' Joey looked surprised.

'Yeah! Blondy!' the big man chuckled. 'On account of I got yeller hair!' He pulled his jet black beard and laughed heartily at his own joke.

But when Joey didn't join in the laugh, the black-haired man scowled suddenly, and gripped Joey's wrist in his powerful fingers. His lip curled back over his big white animal-like teeth as he snarled, 'Got any objections, old-timer?'

Joey cringed. He shook his head dumbly, and his eyes showed such fear that the big man let go of him and gave a contemptuous laugh.

'Okay. Joey and Blondy. That's good enough. And seeing that we're rooming together for a while, let's figure how to get ourselves fixed comfortable here.'

'It's not much of a place,' Joey said timidly. 'And you don't like fish every meal, like I do.'

'Leave it to me,' the man who called himself Blondy told Joey. 'What I don't like, I change.'

And beyond that, he told Joey none of his plans. But after another meal of fish, at sundown, he began to make preparations of a sort that worried Joey. He carefully checked the big revolver that he carried in his belt, as if to be sure that it was ready for use. Then he paced the ground in front of the cave and waited impatiently for darkness to set in.

'You going some place?' Joey asked hopefully.

'Yeah. But I'm coming back. So don't figure you got rid of me. And don't try to run off. Your cooking's a heap better'n I can do. And I like somebody to talk to, even if he's a loony old guy like you! Savvy?'

Joey nodded. He wouldn't try to run away. Even if he had someplace to run to, there was something about the black-browed man that struck terror into his hazy mind.

It was well after midnight when Deputy Terry, making his rounds, noticed that the front door of Sam Moss's store was standing partly open. In twenty years, that was the first time it hadn't been locked and padlocked.

Gun in hand he made a cautious entrance, but there was no one inside. Someone had broken into the cash register, and it was standing open and empty. All around the store, he saw evidence that the place had been looted.

The deputy woke Sam with a phone call, and then reported to Sheriff Bennett. They were both there within a few minutes.

'It's hard to say what all they got,' Sam admitted ruefully, 'but there's some choice lamb chops, at a dollar twenty a pound, missing. And half a dozen tenderloin steaks I was saving for the mayor's wife!'

Carl Bennett pointed to the shelves where gaping spaces showed in the orderly arrangement of cans. 'With that much stuff gone, I'd guess at least a couple of men were in on the theft. And they probably had a car to carry it off in.'

Sam Moss agreed, but Deputy Terry discovered that a sackful of potatoes had been dumped in the store-room, probably so the thief could pile his loot into the empty burlap bag. 'One man could have carried the sackful, but he'd have to be an almighty strong feller and strong as an ox!'

They would have been surprised, at that very moment, to see how closely the deputy's description fitted the thief. Big Blondy was staggering up to the cave, the bulging sack slung over his shoulder.

He dumped it at old Joey's feet, and tin cans by the dozen came rolling out.

Joey stared in amazement touched with fear. 'Must've weighed near a hundred pounds, and you toted it all the way from town!'

Blondy squared his massive shoulders and grinned. 'I sure did, pop! Didn't I tell ya to leave it to me?'

Joey leaned over to examine the contents of the sack. 'Meat! And flour! And *cooked* beans!'

Blondy chuckled. 'We'll be eating high on the hog for a spell,' he boasted. 'And when this is all et up, I'll get us some more fancy food!'

He didn't mention the twenty-odd dollars that he had taken out of the cash register, or a certain other thing he had found there. That was his private business, and there was no reason to tell the old man about it.

In the morning, Sheriff Bennett talked it over with his deputies. 'I'm betting that it was a couple of tramps from the hobo jungle down by the railroad bridge. May-be we ought to drop in on them.'

But when Bennett and a couple of his men drove over

for a quick search of the 'jungle' they found no sign of the food. 'The 'jungle' was a tin-can settlement where the hoboes dropped off the freight trains to rest a few hours or a few days between journeys. Its residents changed continually, as some drifted in and others drifted out.

None of them could remember seeing a big man who could carry a sackful of canned goods. He was most certainly no decent hobo! They were sure of that.

'Where do we look now, boss?' Terry asked. 'Do you really think some campers broke in?'

'I don't know what to think,' Bennett said glumly. 'And I wouldn't know where to start looking!'

13

The Telltale Print

Sam Moss ran out into the street to hail the sheriff as the red car moved through Main Street towards the jail.

'Any sign of him?' he asked anxiously.

'Not yet,' Bennett told him quickly, 'but we haven't given up.'

'There's something I want to show you. Didn't notice it last night, in the dark!' Sam Moss was excited. 'A footprint!'

The car stopped with a jolt. 'Go on to the office,' Bennett told his deputies. 'See if anything's come in. I'll be along.'

Then he hurried around to the rear of the store with Moss. 'Look! He spilled some of the flour, and then stepped on it. Look at the size of that shoe print!'

It was huge, all right. Carl Bennett knelt and measured it. 'Whew! A whopper!' he said softly.

'Big man, hey?' Sam Moss looked half scared. 'I'm glad he waited till I was out of the store before he came in! He must be a giant!'

Carl Bennett frowned. He was trying to remember where he had read or heard about some man who wore an oversize shoe.

Suddenly it came to him. 'Blackie Sanders!' he exclaimed. 'That's where I saw it mentioned! In the Wanted notice for Blackie Sanders!'

'But nobody's seen him around here since that salesman claimed he gave him a lift. And I never did put much stock in *his* story.' Sam Moss didn't want to think that the escaped convict was anywhere around Calverton.

'Oh!' Sam had suddenly remembered. 'There was something I forgot to look for last night.' He led the way inside and to the drawer underneath the cash register. 'I keep a box of shells for my army revolver in this drawer. They're gone – the whole box!'

Sheriff Bennett looked grim. There could be only one reason for the thief to take those shells. He must have a revolver that they would fit! The rumour was that Sanders had stolen a revolver from one of the guards when he escaped from prison. If he was the thief, he would be doubly dangerous now, with the added ammunition.

'Better not mention around town that we think there's a chance it's Blackie Sanders,' he advised the storekeeper. 'If it *was* Sanders, he could have been travelling in a stolen car, and be a long way from here by now. No use getting the whole community in an uproar.'

'But suppose it *is* Sanders, and he's hiding in some empty house or barn?' Sam Moss's voice shook.

'We'll quietly post the farmers to be on the lookout for him, and to let us know the moment they see anyone that might be Sanders.'

So it was that during the next day, Bennett and his men made several visits, singly, to outlying farms. They were careful not to alarm the farmers' families by their questions, but took the menfolk aside each time for private talks.

'Ring us at once, night or day, if you think you've seen him,' Bennett told Paul Martin, when he stopped by the south field where Paul and Uncle Petrie were seeding the last row. 'And you might warn Brunson.'

'You bet we will!' Paul assured him. 'Tonight!'

'Might be better not to frighten Ruth and Timmy,' Carl Bennett suggested, 'though I think I'd keep the youngster out of the woods and close to home for a few days, just in case!'

'Good idea!' Uncle Petrie nodded, then he added soberly, 'though Lassie would take care of him if Sanders or anybody raised a hand to hurt the boy!'

'She might try,' Bennett said grimly, 'but Lassie's teeth wouldn't stand a chance against a revolver. And from Sanders's record, he wouldn't mind using it.'

'I'll see that both Timmy and Lassie stay out of his way!' Paul assured his friend firmly.

It was a gay little cavalcade that drove through the gate of the Brunson farm a couple of hours later.

First came Ruth, at the wheel of the sedan, and with the old maple table teetering crazily on top of the car.

A dozen yards behind the slow-moving sedan, Paul came rumbling along in the shiny new tractor. He had brought his plough along, too, remembering what he had heard about Dave Brunson having to use the old rusty plough that his father had abandoned twenty years ago.

Dave and Meta Brunson came out to meet their visitors as the sedan stopped, and Letty and Pom-Pom ran in from the barn.

Dave hurried down the road to meet Paul and the tractor, his face bright with renewed hope at the sight of it.

Timmy had piled out of the sedan the moment it stopped, and was looking around eagerly for Letty. She came running from the barn, with Pom-Pom at her heels.

'Come see Taffy! I just finished brushing him, an' he looks so pretty!' Letty invited, after the first hellos.

Taffy was stamping impatiently in the barn, as if he wanted to get out and join the party. He nickered a soft welcome when Timmy and Letty came in, and let Timmy pat his nose and scratch his ear without trying to get in a sly nip.

Timmy suggested meeting at the creek tomorrow to try a ride.

But when Letty and Timmy reported their plans to their Dads a few minutes later beside the tractor, they were met with a flat 'No!' from both of them.

'But, Daddy! Why not? You said it was good for me to go riding!' Letty was in tears.

Dave Brunson took her in his arms and mopped the tears away gently. 'Honey, it's only for a few days. Then you can ride anywhere you want to!'

'But we want to go riding tomorrow!' she wailed, and hid her face on his shoulder, sobbing.

'Timmy is going to stay around home for a few days, too,' Paul Martin told her.

Timmy looked astonished. 'But I gotta go hikin' tomorrow. I left somethin' important in the woods, an' I got to get it. I'll come right back, soon as I pick it up.'

Paul Martin shook his head firmly. 'Sorry, son. It'll have to stay where it is, whatever it is. And don't let's have any arguing about it.'

It wasn't often that Dad spoke so sternly to him, so Timmy decided right away that something must really be wrong. He sighed, 'Okay, Dad.'

But he and Letty both forgot their disappointment when they found out that Timmy and Mum and Dad and Uncle Petrie were all staying for a picnic supper under the cherry tree in the Brunsons' side yard.

Later, when Dave Brunson found a few minutes to talk alone to Paul, he found it hard to say how very grateful he was for the loan of the tractor. 'I'm not good at saying thanks,' he said quietly, 'but I think you know it's going to make the difference between staying here and leaving. And when I see how much better Letty seems since we've been here, even in such a short time, I feel as if things were going to work out the way we've hoped.'

'I'm sure they are,' Paul agreed heartily. He looked around the yard. 'You've really cleaned the place up.'

Dave nodded. 'There's still plenty to do, but I plan to tackle it a bit at a time, after I get the planting finished.'

'It'll be good to see your fields under cultivation,' Paul told him with a smile. 'I've always envied you this valley. I guess I just couldn't stand seeing it going to waste.'

Dave sighed. 'They tell me my father had a green thumb, but I'm afraid my fingers are *all* thumbs, and none of them are green!' He laughed ruefully.

'You'll learn by doing, same as the rest of us!' Paul assured him. 'But don't hesitate to call, if you need help.'

'You've done enough, lending me the tractor! From here on in, I hope I can handle the job without leaning on my neighbours!'

There were only a few things that Paul had to show Dave Brunson about the tractor, and then the Martin family was on its way home.

Timmy was asleep in the back seat, with his head against Uncle Petrie's shoulder and Lassie's head in *his* lap.

Ruth stole a look back at him, to be sure he was sound asleep. Then she turned to Paul, who was at the wheel. 'All right. Now tell me why the children can't go riding tomorrow!'

Paul stole a quick look at her. Even in the dim light of the dashboard, he could see she had that look on her face that meant she would keep on asking till he gave her the truth. 'Okay. But don't spread it.' And he told her about the theft of the food and Bennett's suspicion that it was the escaped convict who had stolen it.

When he had finished, she said quietly, 'I hope they find him soon.' And a moment later, 'I can't help feeling sorry for the poor man, no matter what he's done. It must be dreadful to be hunted, and hungry. He's probably living in constant fear of being caught.'

But Ruth Martin was wasting her sympathy. For at that very moment, the man she was pitying was feeling quite at peace with the world. His stomach was full, and he had someone to do the cooking and cleaning up for him, someone to bully, someone who didn't dare dis-

107

obey his orders on penalty of being cuffed around.

He was sitting beside the fire in the old cave, watching old Joey huddle near the draughty mouth of the cave trying to keep warm without the blanket that his visitor had long since taken for his own use.

The intruder felt like talking. 'Hey, old man, what's the law after you for?'

Joey blinked at him sleepily. 'Maybe a lot of things. What's it matter?'

'Just passing the time,' the big man yawned. The fire was burning low, and he looked around for something to throw on it. The newspaper the boys had brought their sandwiches in was lying near at hand. He picked it up and started to throw it on to the dying fire. Then his eyes caught the headline, and he read the article about the escaped convict Blackie Sanders.

When he had finished, he laid the paper aside again, and looked at the sleeping old man through narrowed, speculative eyes. His hand snaked to the revolver that he had laid aside, and he picked it up and cocked it before he called out, 'Hi! Wake up!'

Mumbling protestingly, old Joey turned sleepy eyes on his unwelcome guest. 'Wh-what is it now?' he grumbled. Then his eyes popped wide open as he saw the gun in the big man's hand. It wasn't pointing at him, but it could be, at any moment. 'Wh-what do you want?'

'You ever hear of Blackie Sanders?' the scowling man asked suddenly.

Joey swallowed hard and nodded, unable to speak.

'There's a nice fat reward for anybody that turns him in, ain't there?' The big man leaned forward, glaring at Joey, his hand toying with the pistol.

'There's no use for the gun, Mr Blondy,' the old man said resignedly. 'I'll give up without a fight. You got me, fair and square. I admit I'm Sanders!' He held out empty hands, to show that he was unarmed.

The big man's face was in the shadow, but if Joey could have seen it at that moment, he would have seen an expression on it that was a combination of astonishment and disbelief!

14

Disaster

It took the black-bearded man several seconds to realise that the hazy-minded old fellow really thought that *he* was Blackie Sanders, escaped convict and killer!

And when his slow mind got over the shock, a wide grin spread across his face. Things were working out a lot better than he had expected!

'I don't know how you found out I'm Sanders, but there's no use denying it,' the old man said miserably. 'My mind's kinda hazy, and I've been sort of hoping I was somebody else, but so long as you know me, that's that.'

'Yeah!' The big man nodded, grinning. 'You're him, all right. Took me a while to place you, but all of a sudden I recollected seeing your face in the papers!'

'I suppose you'll be turning me in tomorrow,' Joey sighed. 'Well, maybe it's just as well. Can't keep on hiding for the rest of my life. Might as well get it over with.'

'Who said I figured to turn you in?' Blondy grinned. 'I ain't so friendly with the law boys myself. Only' – his grin disappeared suddenly and a scowl took its place – 'don't you get any ideas about givin' yourself up! I like it here. So we'll let things ride the way they are – *as long as we get along good!*'

There was a look in his beady black eyes that sent a shiver down Joey's spine. 'I didn't have any idea that we wouldn't,' he said hastily.

Lassie came in to wake Timmy up very early the next morning. He was sleepy after being out so late the night before, and tried to hide under the covers. 'Go 'way an' let me sleep!' he called out from under the blanket. But Lassie jumped up on the bed, took the blanket in her teeth, and tugged it off him.

Timmy grabbed for the blanket, but she was too quick for him. She pulled it off the bed and out of his reach.

Then she stood off and barked at him.

'Okay!' Timmy sat up and rubbed his eyes. 'Only, there's no school until next week, an' I coulda slept lots longer.' But even while he was saying it, he remembered something. 'Hey, that's right, Lassie! We're going out to the Brunsons' this morning! Golly! I nearly forgot!'

'Well, Lassie and I didn't forget!' Ruth Martin laughed at him from the doorway. 'Hurry up and get washed and dressed. Your breakfast will be ready in five minutes!'

'You bet!' Timmy swung out of bed cheerfully and dashed for the bathroom.

But Ruth caught him by the shoulder as he started to go by her. 'Put on your old cords, in case. Letty's dad

111

says you may ride Taffy around the yard!' she reminded him.

And the day started out to be a happy one for both the Martin family and the Brunsons.

Timmy could hardly wait to arrive at the Brunson farm, and he found Letty and Pom-Pom just as excited as he and Lassie were. Letty's father had left some time ago on the tractor, to start his ploughing, but he had made Letty promise not to take the pony away from the farmyard.

Taffy was tied to the porch rail, and Timmy hadn't the least bit of trouble mounting into the saddle from the steps. He gripped the reins hard at first, but as he got used to the saddle, he relaxed and even urged Taffy to trot.

Letty was delighted, and generously let him ride several times around the yard before she took her turn at riding.

They were having so much fun with Taffy, that for once Timmy forgot all about Lassie being there.

Pom-Pom had to look for something exciting to do. His bright eyes followed the pony in its trot around the yard. He seemed to be trying to decide if it would be worth the effort to run after the big brown creature and nip at its heels. But he had done that before, and narrowly escaped being kicked for it. He would have to find something safer to do.

A faint, far-off, familiar sound brought him to his feet, sniffing. A little while ago, he had had a wonderful time barking at that big, slow-moving monster as it clanked its way out of the yard. He had kept after it, doing his best to nip those strange-looking wheels-that-weren't-wheels.

112

Now he heard the monster again. He growled threateningly. It wasn't a very ferocious growl, but it was the best he could manage, and it made Lassie sit up and look at him inquiringly.

'Come on!' Pom-Pom barked at Lassie. 'Help me drive off the monster!'

Lassie got up slowly. She looked over towards the porch. Timmy and Letty were going to ride double now, and no one seemed interested in what Lassie was doing.

'Come on! Hurry, you slowpoke!' Pom-Pom barked reprovingly. So Lassie trotted slowly towards him, with only one last glance back at Timmy. Then they ran down the road together.

Dave Brunson was rather proud of all the work he had been able to do in one morning with the borrowed tractor. At first, it had seemed an unwieldy monster. But as the morning wore on, he had become quite expert at turning corners and keeping his furrows straight.

In his mind's eye he could already see the tall rows of corn swaying in the summer breezes.

Now he heard the far-off yipping of Pom-Pom and with it the deeper barking of Lassie.

Suddenly the barking was closer. Dave didn't pay too much attention to it, until something small and white flashed into sight directly ahead of the tractor. It was Pom-Pom, and apparently he was intent on destroying the strange monster. He was running straight towards it.

'Shoo! Get away! Go, Pom-Pom!' Dave Brunson shouted, waving his arm at the tiny dog in his path. But Pom-Pom kept coming.

Out of the side of his eye he saw Lassie coming at a fast run at an angle, as if she hoped to run the puppy

8

out of the way of the tractor. But she was too far away to help now. There was only one thing to do – swerve the tractor quickly to one side. And even then he couldn't be sure he would miss the tiny white puppy.

He gripped the wheel and swung the tractor over as sharply as he could. But in his panic, he pressed down hard on the gas pedal. The tractor not only swung around, but shot forward in a sudden burst of speed that sent it crashing through the fence and down an embankment into the rock-filled gully beyond.

Dave barely had time to jump from the high seat of the tractor, before it turned over and landed with a crash among the rocks. He fell a few feet from it.

He became conscious of a sharp pain in his arm. As he staggered to his feet, he tried to lift the arm and found that he couldn't. It was badly broken.

He felt dizzy, suddenly, and sat down. And when he tried to get to his feet again, the pain in his arm was so bad that everything went suddenly dark and he pitched forward on his face, in a dead faint.

Up on the edge of the field, Lassie and Pom-Pom stared down at the wreck. Pom-Pom barked hysterically at the fallen monster, but Lassie looked down at the man who was lying motionless a few feet from the tractor.

Then Lassie made a careful descent to Dave Brunson's side. When she got there, she sniffed at him and whined a little, touching him gently with her paw to wake him. When it didn't bring a response, she barked urgently. And when he still lay quiet, she seemed to decide that it was time to do something about it.

She picked up the wide-brimmed straw hat that had fallen off Brunson's head, and with it in her teeth, she climbed up out of the gully and started off at top speed towards the distant farmhouse.

Ruth Martin saw Lassie come running into the farmyard carrying Dave Brunson's hat in her mouth.

'Now what has that silly dog found?' she laughed, and pointed out the window. 'Somebody's hat!'

Timmy and Letty had been sitting on the steps, resting after their pony rides, when they saw Lassie come running into the yard. 'Here, girl! Whatcha got?' Timmy called.

But when Lassie brought it over to them, put it down at Timmy's feet, and barked loudly, Letty told Timmy with surprise, 'Why, it's Daddy's work hat!'

And at the same time. Meta, staring out of the kitchen window, recognised it also. 'She has my husband's hat!' she exclaimed. 'How on earth did she get hold of it?'

Ruth watched Lassie run away a few feet, and then come back to bark at Timmy and Letty. She had seen the handsome and intelligent big collie act like that before. She guessed that Lassie was trying to get the children to follow her. Maybe something was wrong . . . 'Let's go see what Lassie's fussing about!' she suggested.

'She wants us to go with her someplace!' Timmy ran up. 'Can we go, Mum?'

'Why don't we all go?' Ruth suggested quickly. 'Maybe Letty's daddy has finished the ploughing and sent her to bring us so we can see how nice the field looks!'

So they started out to follow Lassie, who kept running ahead and barking back at them. Long before they came in sight of the empty field with its broken fence, Ruth guessed that there had been some kind of accident.

By the time that Meta reached the edge of the field

and scrambled down to her husband's side, he was conscious once more, and white-faced with pain from his broken arm. And Pom-Pom, snuggled close to him, was growling defiance at the fallen tractor in the ditch, warning it not to dare make a threatening move or he would tear it to pieces.

Dave managed to stagger to his feet with Meta's help, but he had to lean on her to keep from collapsing. Together they stared at the badly damaged tractor.

'Well, this time I've really done it!' Dave said bitterly. 'Smashed myself and Martin's tractor at the same time!'

Ruth spoke as she hurried down to join them. 'Don't worry about the tractor. I'm sure it's fully insured against any kind of accident! The important thing is to get you to the doctor right away.'

'I hope you're right about the insurance,' Dave said miserably a little later, as they all rode in the sedan towards Dr Wilson's office in Calverton. He was in a great deal of pain, but the damage to the tractor he had borrowed gave him more worry than his own injury.

'Of course, I am!' Ruth called back cheerfully from the front seat.

Dave Brunson smiled painfully. 'I'm lucky that he thinks that way. I hate to think of what it is going to cost to repair that tractor!'

15

Defeat

It was a grim-faced group of Calverton men who made a search of the surrounding country to try to find the man who had burglarised Sam Moss's store. Most of them were armed with shotguns, and only the deputies and sheriff had revolvers.

The searchers split into parties of two, and each covered a section of territory. They went into every barn and shed, and searched every empty house. But there was no cache of stolen food to be found, and no trace of the thief.

Twice during the morning, a pair of searchers moved through the deep woods, on their way from one farm to another in a more remote location. And twice, they were watched from deep in the tangled brush by the black-bearded man with a revolver in his belt. He had a very good hunch they were looking for him, and he was ready to kill rather than be captured. So it was a good thing for them that they had no idea he was close at hand.

He watched them move away and then he went back to the cave to old Joey. Joey was getting ready to go fishing, but Blondy stopped him.

'We got plenty to eat here. I don't want any fish,' he told Joey.

Joey sighed and set the fishing pole inside the cave. 'Had my mouth set for fish, but I guess tomorrow's just as good.' And he went inside to start the fire for their next meal.

It was a couple of hours later that Paul Martin, riding in Sam Moss's pickup trick with Uncle Petrie and two more of the searchers, saw his own sedan parked in front of the Calverton Hospital.

In a flash, he was out of the truck and running over to the sedan.

Dr Wilson came out of the operating room just as Paul joined Meta and Ruth. 'There's nothing to worry about, Mrs Brunson,' he explained. 'Your husband has a rather bad fracture, but he'll be as good as new in a few weeks.'

'A few weeks!' She was dismayed and worried.

'As a matter of fact, I may let him come home in a couple of days if you'll promise not to let him try to work!'

But when Dave Brunson came home two days later, he had no desire to go back to ploughing. He had decided to give up and take his family back to the city.

He felt bitter about his failure. 'I don't know why I ever thought I could run a farm. I was a fool to try,' he told Meta, as they sat on the porch late that day.

Meta looked out across the orchard and sighed. A

short time ago she had been the one who didn't want to stay here and try to make a go of farming. Now, when she had found a friend in Ruth Martin and had made plans to join the rest of the Calverton wives and mothers in their various neighbourly activities, she had to give them up.

'Can't we stay a little longer?' she asked. 'Letty likes it so much here. And people are so kind!'

'I wish we could,' Dave looked glum, 'but by the time I can get back to work, it will be too late to do any planting. Summer will be here, and the sun will shrivel the young plants.'

Meta was silent, and Dave sighed as he saw her disappointed look.

'Do you suppose we could come back next year – and try again?' she asked timidly.

Dave shook his head. 'It's no use,' he said wearily. 'The best thing we can do is to sell the place and go.'

'Sell it?' Meta was shocked.

So was Letty. She could hardly believe what she was hearing. She didn't *want* to believe it.

'We have no choice,' her father was saying. 'After I've paid Dr Wilson, there won't be enough left in the bank to keep us going more than a month or so.'

'Couldn't we ask him to wait till later?'

'Did he ask *me* to wait when I broke this arm? Doctors have to live and pay their own bills!' Dave felt strongly about that.

'I suppose so,' Meta sighed. 'Will we be leaving soon?'

'I'll put the farm in the hands of the real estate people for immediate sale. I'm sure they'll find a buyer right away.' He tried to be cheerful, but it was hard work.

119

Inside, Letty clapped her hand over her mouth to keep back a cry of protest and ran to her room.

Once she got there, she climbed up on her bed and let loose a flood of tears into her pillow. She didn't want to go away. She hated the city. She was so happy here. The whole world was against her. She hated everybody. She wouldn't go! She would run away!

There was a faint scratching noise at her closed door and a sad little whimpering.

Letty slid off the bed and ran to open the door. A small white object flashed past her and leaped up on to the bed. 'Oh, Pom-Pom!' She gently put her arms around the puppy. 'I know you'll just hate being in the city, same as me.'

But Pom-Pom wriggled away and jumped down off the bed, to run to the window and whine excitely.

Letty dashed the tears away. 'What's the matter?'

There was a pleasant surprise down there. It was the Martin car, and Timmy and Lassie were just erupting out of it as Mr and Mrs Martin walked towards the front porch.

When the greetings were over, Timmy suggested, 'Hey, let's go see Taffy. I brought him an apple.'

'May we, Mummy, please?' Letty asked eagerly. 'He loves apples!'

'All right, dear,' Meta nodded.

So Letty and Timmy, and the two dogs, had a race to see who could get to the barn first, and Lassie won. ''Cause she's got four legs an' we only have two,' Timmy apologised to a breathless Letty.

Pom-Pom brought up the rear. 'You'll have to learn to run faster,' Letty scolded him. Then she remembered suddenly that they wouldn't be doing any running and racing in the city. 'Oh, dear!' Tears filled her eyes.

'Hey!' Timmy went over to her, scowling. 'Whatcha cryin' about?' And when Letty had wailed out the bad news that they were selling the farm and going back to the city, Timmy didn't really believe it. But when Letty insisted it was true, Timmy looked almost as woebegone as she did.

'We've got to go away,' she said miserably. 'Daddy has no money.'

The Martin family was up early the next morning. Paul had promised Dave Brunson he would go to the real estate office and tell Thad Smith that the farm was up for sale. He hated to do it, but Dave was positive that he was all done with farming. And considering the hard luck he had had, Paul could hardly blame him.

'I wish we could take the place off their hands,' Ruth said soberly. 'But I guess we have all we can handle here.'

'You guess right,' Paul agreed. 'Money – money – money – why can't we grow it on trees?'

"If we could, I'd like to plant a money tree in the Brunsons' front yard!' Uncle Petrie said wryly. 'Sure hate to see them move away again. Why can't that Brunson boy have the know-how his pa did?'

'Don't forget he left before he had a chance to get it! You don't inherit that,' Paul reminded him. 'You learn it!'

16

Bad News

Ruth was busy in the kitchen, stirring something in a pot on the stove. Uncle Petrie was finishing his lunch. And out in the yard Paul had the tyres off the sedan, changing them around so they would wear more evenly.

'This chicken stew is almost done, but from the looks of the car out there, I'm afraid I won't get it out to Dave Brunson for hours,' Ruth told Uncle Petrie.

'I s'pose I could take it over in the pickup,' Uncle Petrie offered reluctantly, 'but I was countin' on layin' a coat of paint on that shed this afternoon.'

'Mum! Can I take it on my bike? It'd ride just fine in my wire basket!' Timmy offered.

'I don't see why not, now the burglar's not in our area anymore,' Ruth agreed. 'But don't stay too long. The radio says that storm is almost here!'

'I'll be back in a hurry,' Timmy promised, 'long before it starts raining!'

But some big drops the size of pennies had started

falling even before Timmy got to the Brunsons' valley with Lassie beside him and the stew riding safely in the covered pot in the wire basket.

Meta was delighted with the thoughtful offering, and Dave's gloomy face lighted up at the sight of the tasty food. 'They're fine people, the Martins,' he said quietly. 'We would have gotten to be good friends, I know.'

'Dave,' Meta asked, 'couldn't we *mortgage* the place, and stay on?'

He shook his head sadly. 'Paul thought of that, and he talked to the bankers yesterday. They reminded him that without a crop, I'd have no way of meeting payments.' He made a wry grimace. 'So – they had to turn us down.' His hand was on hers. 'I don't want to leave here either, dear. But we have no other choice.'

Timmy knew, as the raindrops began coming down more heavily, that he and Lassie really should be starting for home. But he had to go look for Letty and spend a few minutes petting Taffy before he left.

He and Lassie found Letty trying to convince Pom-Pom that he shouldn't be afraid of falling off Taffy's back. But every time that Letty lifted him into Taffy's saddle and told him to stay there, the white puppy jumped right down again, and ran into a dark corner of the barn to hide.

'I guess I'll never get him trained like the poodles in the circus,' she confided to Timmy after they had all said hello to each other.

'Maybe if Lassie showed him how, he wouldn't be scared,' Timmy suggested.

But that was one time that Lassie refused firmly to take orders. She backed away in spite of all Timmy's coaxing and stern commands, and ran over to hide in the same dark corner where Pom-Pom had taken refuge.

That made Letty giggle, but the giggle stopped suddenly as they heard a big vehicle come creaking into the yard and stop outside the barn. 'Wonder who that is.'

Timmy and she both went to look out into the rain-filled yard.

'Oh, it's the man who sold Taffy to us!' she exclaimed.

It was a big van, and on the side of it, large letters proclaimed that it belonged to the Elite Dog and Pony Show. It was painted red, white and blue, in all sorts of curlicues and patterns, with a fine gilt trim, sort of ginger-bready and fancy.

'Maybe he's got another pony to sell!' Timmy's eyes sparkled with excitement. 'Maybe my folks would buy it!'

'Guess I'll go find out!' Letty announced. 'And if he has a cute one, I'll ask Daddy to tell *your* dad you'd like to have it!'

'Yeah! I guess that's better than *me* askin',' Timmy decided. 'But I sure would like to know.' He looked longingly at the wagon, from which they could hear various thumpings that seemed to indicate that there were ponies inside.

The rain was really coming down now, and there was a big clap of thunder that seemed to come from right overhead.

'Golly! I guess I better get on home right away!' Timmy decided hastily. 'I'll come over tomorrow and find out what happened!'

Letty pulled off her apron and threw it over her head like a shawl. Then she picked up Pom-Pom and cuddled him under it with her. 'Okay! See you tomorrow!' she told Timmy and dashed for the house.

Timmy turned up his collar, whistled Lassie to him, and ran for his bike. A moment later, he was headed up the lane, homeward bound.

Letty came into the kitchen, a little wet from the short run in the heavy rain. There was a brisk little fire in the old stove, and she set Pom-Pom down in front of it while she got an old towel to dry off his soft white coat.

The door to the living room was open, and Letty could hear the voices of her father and mother and the pony man. At first she didn't pay much attention, but suddenly something the man said made her stop and listen.

'I can take the pony tomorrow,' the man was saying in his harsh, loud voice. 'I can't wait any longer than that, because I'm booked for Capitol City Fair Grounds this weekend and I won't be back this way.'

'Couldn't you leave him here just a few days more? I'd like some time to explain to our little girl that we can't take him to the city with us!' It was her mother's voice.

'Lady, it's tomorrow or nothin'!' the harsh voice said. 'I'm giving you more than the critter's worth, as it is. I sold him to you in the first place because I couldn't teach him any tricks. I'm doin' you a favour buying him back.'

'What time tomorrow?' That was her father speaking. His voice sounded tired.

'Early. I wanta be on the road by eight or eight thirty.'

'All right. He'll be in the barn, waiting.'

125

'I'll bring the cash with me,' the man said, and Letty heard the scrape of a chair on the bare floor.

She snatched up Pom-Pom, bundled him in the old towel, and ran to the door in the hall. She closed it softly behind her as the pony show man came into the kitchen with Meta Brunson.

'I'll give you a fair price for any tack you've bought for him, saddle and whatnot. You won't be needing it any more,' the man told Meta. Then, in a kinder voice, he added, 'Too bad things didn't work out, ma'am.'

Meta looked surprised. 'Why, thank you!' she said, 'that's very kind of you.'

And when the gruff-spoken showman had driven the big van out of the yard through the pouring rain, she went back to Dave, in the living room, and told him, 'People *are* friendlier in the country, aren't they? Oh, I wish we could stay!'

'So do I, dear,' Dave told her softly. 'So do I.' But there was no hope in his voice, only resignation.

'I think I'd better go tell Letty about the pony now,' Meta said. It wasn't going to be easy to do, she thought, but she had to be told.

Letty was in her own room, looking out at the driving rain, with Pom-Pom on her lap. She took the news about Taffy very calmly, much to her mother's relief.

'I guess he *would* be a nuisance in the city,' Letty agreed soberly, after Meta had made a full explanation.

Meta put her arms around Letty affectionately. 'Darling, I'm so glad you understand. We'd never sell Taffy if there were only some way we could keep him.'

'I know, Mummy,' Letty nodded. She patted her mother on the shoulder. 'It's not your fault.' And Meta, with her own eyes brimming, couldn't see a trace of tears in Letty's.

She went back to Dave with a lighter heart, to tell him how bravely Letty had taken the bad news. 'She didn't even cry. And I know how much that pony means to her!'

But if Letty hadn't cried then, she made up for it during the long night, before the first streaks of dawn showed in the rain-swept sky.

All night the rain had kept up without slackening, and it was still coming down now in a steady downpour that threatened to flood the lowlands and overflow the creeks.

Invalided Dave Brunson and his wife slept soundly in the grey dawn. But Letty moved hastily about her room, getting dressed for a last ride. She had made up her mind to it during the long night.

Quietly, she let herself out of the house and ran to the barn. But quiet as she was, someone else had watched her every move. And as she hurriedly saddled up Taffy, Pom-Pom waited close at hand to go along with them, and Letty couldn't make him go back to the house.

When she was ready to leave, she picked up the white puppy and dropped him into the empty stall and closed the half-door on him. 'I'll be back, Pom-Pom darling.'

17

The Runaway

It was starting to rain again, but gently now, as Letty rode her pony down the road in the direction of Timmy Martin's house. She was sorry that she had had to lock up poor little Pom-Pom, but she planned to be back again in a couple of hours to let him out.

The ride seemed to be endless, in the grey early morning, but finally she came in sight of the Martins' white fence, and then soon she was in the farmyard. And she had been riding less than an hour.

She rode towards the barn, expecting that Timmy would come charging out at any moment to meet her. But even Lassie wasn't anywhere to be seen.

Timmy was still fast asleep in his room, and Ruth was the only Martin awake so far, on this rainy morning.

Lassie, lying on her blanket beside Timmy's bed, lifted her head and listened. Then she padded over to the open window, pushed aside the curtain with her nose, and stared out. A moment later, she had leaped through the window and was running across the farmyard to greet the tired, wet little girl who was dismounting from her pony.

Her bark of greeting was loud and cheerful, and it brought Timmy stumbling out of bed and to the window, to see what Lassie had found to bark at so early in the morning. One look, and he was wide awake and rushing to get his clothes on.

Two minutes later he was out of the house, fully dressed except for one shoe, which he just couldn't wait to put on before he went to say hello. 'Hey! What are you doing here?' he demanded, waving the shoe at her.

'I brought Taffy for you,' she told him.

'For *me?*' Timmy was astonished.

She nodded solemnly. 'We have to sell him. So I thought maybe your folks would buy him for you.' She was trying hard to be brave, but her voice broke in spite of herself. 'That pony man wants to take him away this morning, so I had to bring him over early.'

'Golly, I'd sure like to own him!' Timmy stroked the pony's soft brown nose.

'If you buy him, maybe I can come see him sometimes,' Letty said, laying her cheek against the pony's neck.

Ruth Martin leaned out of the kitchen window. 'Letty! Where did you come from at this hour of the morning? How about some breakfast with us?'

Letty was glad to be inside the warm, pleasant kitchen and out of the rain. But she didn't care about any breakfast, right away. She wouldn't be hungry till she

9

knew that Taffy was going to be safe with Timmy and his folks.

Paul Martin came in as she was explaining her errand, and he looked very serious about it. 'I'm sorry, honey,' he told her, 'but your daddy has already agreed to sell Taffy to the pony man. That makes it a promise, and the pony man is probably counting on using Taffy for his act. You can't ask your dad to go back on his promise. It wouldn't be fair to the pony man.'

'But I don't want him to have Taffy!' she protested. 'He'll take him away where I'll never see him any more!'

'He has a right to, once he's made a deal to buy him,' Ruth explained gently. 'Can't you see that?'

'I s'pose so,' she admitted tearfully. 'But he doesn't like Taffy. He doesn't think he's smart. Maybe he'll even b-beat him when Taffy can't learn tricks. Oh, please take him! He'll be so happy here!'

'I'm sorry, Letty,' Timmy's father told her, 'but you'd better take him back home now. The pony man will be looking for him.'

Letty saw from their faces that it was no use. She picked up her raincoat and started hastily towards the door.

'Wait, dear. You're not going without some warm food inside you,' Ruth told her firmly, 'and then Uncle Petrie can drive you home in the pickup, and Taffy can trot along behind it.'

Letty backed towards the door. 'I have to see how Taffy is, first. I'll – I'll be back!' She turned suddenly and flew out the door into the rain.

Lassie ran to the door and looked after her, barking.

'She's comin' back, Lassie,' Timmy assured the collie. 'Whatcha fussin' for?'

But Lassie kept on barking, and when Timmy ran to the door to look out, he was just in time to see Letty riding out of the yard at a fast trot. 'Mum! She's riding away!' he shouted.

'Oh, dear!' Ruth was just a little annoyed at the stubborn child. 'At least she could have let us take her home!'

But Letty wasn't going home. When she had gone a mile or so on the dirt road, she cut off suddenly into the woods.

The rain was coming down steadily now, and the flash of distant lightning promised even more storm.

She rode along the narrow woodland path, so familiar now to her. Taffy was a little skittish when the thunder rolled, off in the distance, but she patted his neck and told him soothingly, 'Don't be scared. It's only thunder.'

When she came to the creek, she noticed that there was a lot more water in it than usual, and the water was racing along at great speed. She didn't notice that there was a place just ahead where the water had cut into the bank.

Taffy stumbled, struggled to regain his footing, and neighed in terror as he felt the soft bank giving way under his feet and throwing him off balance.

Letty sawed at the reins, trying to pull him back to safety, but she herself slipped in the saddle, her foot came out of the stirrup and she fell and rolled halfway down the bank.

If she hadn't been wet enough before, she certainly was now, as she scrambled back up the bank with the rain lashing against her face.

131

Through the heavy brush, she could just make out a glimpse of the brown pony, and then he disappeared. She ran as fast as she could, through the tangle of bushes and saplings, calling 'Taffy! Come back!' But she didn't get another sight of him.

When she finally stopped, bramble torn, soaking, and tearful, she was lost.

The woods were dark here. She had never been this deep in the tangled brush. And the murky sky overhead made the place spooky and frightening.

'Taffy!' she called. But she knew he wouldn't come.

She sat down on a rock and cried, and her tears mingled with the rain until, suddenly, a most welcome shaft of sunlight beamed down and spread over the rock. The warmth of it stopped the chattering of her teeth, but she huddled there forlornly, too frightened to try to find her way back to the creek and the familiar path along the top of the bank. She had dropped her riding glove somewhere, but she didn't bother to look for it, in her terrified misery.

The pony man was driving his big van into the farmyard when Meta came to the kitchen door to see who it was so early in the morning. She had half forgotten that he had said he would be there first thing in the morning.

'Oh dear! He *is* early!' she told Dave, frowning. 'Do you think we should wake up Letty so she can say goodbye to Taffy?'

Dave Brunson, in his pyjamas and with his broken arm in a sling, shook his head. 'Better not. If Taffy's gone when she gets up, it might be easier on her.'

She agreed soberly. Then Dave slipped a raincoat over his shoulders and went out to meet the pony man and to deliver Taffy and the harness to him in exchange for the money.

Meta tiptoed up to Letty's room and softly pushed the door open. If Letty was awake, she would need her mother's arms to comfort her over the loss of her pet.

But Letty wasn't there!

Meta thought she knew where to find her. She went slowly downstairs and out to the barn. But there was no sign of her there, either. And Taffy's stall was empty except for Pom-Pom, who barked indignantly at them and rushed out to jump all over them when they opened the half door.

The pony man was angry. 'What kind of a deal is this? Where's the pony?'

'We don't know any more about it than you do,' Dave Brunson said sharply. 'The child has probably taken him for a last ride. She'll be back soon.'

'Well, I don't have time to wait for her,' the scowling showman told them. 'I'm calling off the deal. I didn't want him much anyhow. I was just trying to do you folks a favour by taking him off your hands.'

Dave and Meta watched him drive the big pony van out of the yard, and for a moment neither of them spoke. Then Dave smiled crookedly. 'I'm sort of glad it didn't work out, after all. We'll find somebody to buy him, I'm sure!'

Meta nodded, smiling back at him. Then she sobered. Something caught her eye far down the road behind him, and her face went white. 'Dave! Look!'

He wheeled and stared, and his own face turned the colour of putty. Taffy was trotting towards them. He looked very perky and proud of himself, with his mane and tail flowing in the breeze, but he was caked with mud halfway up his legs, and the saddle was hanging way over to one side. The reins were dragging on the ground.

'Something's happened to my baby!' Meta cried out, and for a moment it looked as if she might be going to fall in a faint. Dave caught her with his well arm, and held her.

'Meta!' He spoke loudly to make her stop her hysterical sobbing. 'Stop that! Maybe she dismounted and Taffy ran away! You know what a tricky fellow he is!'

'But – the twisted saddle! I know she's lying in the road somewhere, badly hurt!'

'You don't know anything of the sort,' he insisted. He was stilling his own fears while he tried to calm hers.

'I'm going to find her!' she announced, trying to wrench free and run up the road. But Dave held her firmly.

'Wait, dear! We don't know what direction Taffy came from. We can't just rush blindly around, and miss her. The best thing for us to do is to get the car out and we'll try to trace Taffy's hoofprints back along the road. Maybe we'll meet her coming along on foot!'

'Oh, I hope so!' Meta rushed to the house to get the car keys and start the search.

But when she came out with the keys, Paul Martin and Uncle Petrie were driving up in their truck. She ran to them.

'Letty's missing!' she called excitedly.

Uncle Petrie spoke under his breath to Paul. 'Doggone! You were right, Paul. You figured she'd run off with that cussed pony rather'n give him up!'

Paul nodded with a grave expression. 'Don't worry, Meta,' he told the young mother. 'We'll find her fast.'

He jumped out of the truck and told Uncle Petrie, 'Get Carl and a couple of his boys. We'll do this right.' He had noticed the twisted saddle right away, and was afraid that Meta's fears of Letty's having been hurt were going to be realised.

'I'm going along!' Meta announced, but Paul caught Dave's eye and shook his head warningly.

Dave understood. He put his arm around Meta's waist and told her quietly. 'You'd only be in the way, dear. Better wait right here till they bring her back!'

'That's right, ma'am,' Uncle Petrie leaned out of the truck and managed to give her a reassuring grin. 'The young'un will be needing a good hot bath to get this mud off, judgin' by Taffy's looks!'

A few minutes later, Uncle Petrie had roared off down the road to get the sheriff and a couple of his deputies, and Paul and Dave were setting out to back-track the pony to find out where he had come from.

The pony's trail – clear in the damp, sandy road – came from the woods. But once they had followed it that far, it was lost in the damp fallen leaves. They were stopped.

Paul Martin cupped his hands around his mouth and called 'Letty! Letty!' turning from one direction to the other. But there was no answer.

It wouldn't be easy finding her, wherever she was.

Deep in the tangled brush, beyond a series of low hills, Letty was still sitting on the sunny rock. She felt warm now and more hopeful of finding her way home again. She was pretty sure that Taffy would head straight for the barn, the bad little fellow! And she wondered if the pony show man would still be waiting to take Taffy away with him. She guessed he would be.

She heard something crashing through the brush in her direction, and she jumped up and stared around her in fright. It sounded awfully big – like a bear, perhaps!

Now she located the direction of the smashing, crashing noise. It was off to one side, but she couldn't see anything yet. Maybe there was still time to hide.

She darted behind a boulder and hardly dared to look out, as the noise came closer, but she ventured one tiny peek.

Now the brush crasher had come into sight. It was a big man with a bristling blackbeard and the biggest feet she thought she had ever seen! He had two dead rabbits slung over his shoulder, and there was a revolver in his belt.

She held her breath and shrank closer to the boulder. But the man stalked on past her – hardly two yards away – and crashed his way into the darkness of the woods.

For a moment, she was tempted to call out and run after him. She thought he might be able to tell her which way to go to get safely out of the woods again.

But something held her back. Perhaps it was the bushy black beard, or the small animal-like eyes. More probably, it was the sight of those poor little rabbits!

Whatever it was, she didn't call to him. And it was just as well that she hadn't!

18

Lassie Helps Out

The black-bearded man who called himself Blondy, to confuse old Joey, was getting ready to pull out. The heavy rain had made the cave damp and miserable, and old Joey had been more than ever wrapped in his own silence.

Joey watched the big man toss the dead rabbits on the ground near the fire, but he made no move to start to skin them and get them ready for the stew that Blondy wanted.

'What's eating you now?' the black-bearded one snarled. 'Hurry up! I'm getting hungry.'

Joey eyed the rabbits gloomily and shook his head. 'Ain't going to touch them. That little feller with the dark splotch on his shoulder was a particular friend of mine. Fed right out of my hand. You can cook him yourself.'

'Why, you crazy old galoot! I oughta –' The big man

137

glared at Joey, and his hand hovered over the butt of his revolver. Then, suddenly, he laughed and relaxed. 'Okay. I'll cook your pal. And I'll make a good meal for myself. And what's left, I'll take along with me.'

'Where you going?' Old Joey's eyes brightened.

'Far away as I can get, old man. I'll be as batty as you are, if I stick around much longer!'

'You aren't figuring to turn me in to the law, are you?' Joey asked fearfully.

'Not a chance!' big Blondy laughed. Then he grinned at the old man, and asked mockingly, 'You recollect any of your killings yet, Blackie?'

Old Joey shivered and shook his head firmly. 'Can't say I do. I try. But my mind won't go beyond the hospital!'

The big man laughed. 'Well, seeing I'm leaving you right after the rain's cleared up and the going is easier, I got to tell you a big joke.'

'A joke? Who on?' Joey eyed him curiously.

'On you, old-timer!' He leaned back against the cave wall and grinned at Joey. 'Y'see, Joey, you ain't Blackie Sanders at all. You're just a poor old hobo that probably fell off a freight car and got a bad bump on the head. You ain't *anybody*!'

Old Joey looked startled. 'But you recognised me –'

Blondy chuckled and waved it aside. 'I'm a great kidder, old man. I was ribbing you.'

'But, Blondy --' Joey was bewildered now.

The big man interrupted with a laugh. 'The name is Sanders. And the front handle is Blackie.'

Joey blinked at him, speechless. It was too much for him.

'There's no harm telling you now,' the big man

138

grinned. 'I'll be pulling out real soon.' Then he scowled suddenly and leaned close to Joey, gripping the front of Joey's shirt in one hairy hand. 'But till I do, you're going to stay real close at hand. Don't get any notions about running to the law. If you try to make a break, I'll forget my manners.'

Uncle Petrie had lost no time getting Sheriff Bennett on the telephone from the Martin farm. Within half an hour, Bennett and two deputies had arrived to start the search for Letty.

Timmy stood watching, with Lassie beside him, as the men piled into the official-looking car.

Ruth called, 'Good luck!' but Timmy suddenly made up his mind and ran to the side of the car.

'I bet Lassie could find her! Do you want us to go along?' he asked eagerly.

'No, Timmy,' Carl Bennett said quickly, 'but thanks just the same. I'm sure we can find her without Lassie.'

Timmy stood watching the car drive off, and he patted Lassie's head. 'They weren't very polite to you,' he told her solemnly, 'but *I* know you could find her easy.'

Ruth saw his expression, and she called out cheerfully, 'Why don't you go on over to see Boomer? You haven't played with him for days! I have to phone his mother about something else. Shall I tell her you're coming over?' She thought that Timmy was worrying about Letty, and it would do him good to be with Boomer till Letty was safely home with her folks.

'I guess so.' Timmy wasn't enthusiastic. 'Come on, Lassie.' He went to get his bike, and a few minutes later Ruth saw him ride off along the muddy main road towards the Bates farm, with Lassie running by his side.

She felt relieved. Now Timmy wouldn't take it into his head to tag along after the men.

But it didn't work out the way she expected.

Boomer was glad to see his pal Timmy, and excited when Timmy told him of Letty's disappearance.

'I told Sheriff Bennett Lassie could find her,' Timmy complained, stroking Lassie, 'but he didn't believe me.'

'Hey! Why don't we just go anyhow, and let Lassie look for her? We know a lot of places in the dark part of the woods that the sheriff doesn't know, I betcha!'

'Yeah!' Timmy's eyes sparkled, 'and if we don't find her right off, we can go talk to Joey, and ask if he's seen anybody around!'

'Let's go!' Boomer ran into the shed and wheeled out his bike. 'We can ride part way, till the brush gets too thick. And look!' He pulled a small whistle out of his pocket and showed it to Timmy. He gave a couple of shrill toots on it. 'If we get far apart, I'll whistle and you can come where *I* am.'

That being agreed on, they set off briskly, pedalling as hard as they could, uphill and down. And in a very short time, they were well into the woods.

Lassie watched them dismount and hide their bikes under the bushes. She sniffed the air inquiringly, as they didn't seem to know which direction to start towards.

A faint, tiny sound of barking came to her keen ears, and she sat up, whining softly.

Now the boys could hear it, too. 'It's Pom-Pom!' Timmy shouted. 'Come on! I bet Letty's with him!'

He led the way, crashing through the brush, in the

direction of the faint barking, but Lassie pushed ahead of him after a few yards, in her usual protective position. If any danger should be ahead, she would meet it first.

When they came in sight of Pom-Pom, the puppy was balancing dizzily on a fallen tree trunk out in the middle of the rushing creek. The poor little animal was so wet that its usually fluffy coat was clinging tightly to its plump body, and its frantic little barks were turning into wails of terror, as its tiny nails slipped on the wet wood.

Just as they came in sight of it, the puppy gave a despairing howl, slipped off the trunk, and was carried roughly downstream. It disappeared in the turbulent water.

The boys stared helplessly after it, but Lassie didn't waste a second. She plunged into the rushing water, and let herself be carried downstream.

She kept her head up and watched the water closely for a glimpse of the puppy, as she was borne along. For just a second, a small white body was tossed out of the water, as the current swerved around the foot of a rock. A second, but it was enough for Lassie!

She struck out with all her strength towards the spot where the puppy had appeared, and the boys, watching helplessly, saw her disappear into the water for a moment and then emerge, carrying a white bundle in her teeth.

They ran along the shore, and met her as she struggled up the muddy bank with the soaking wet, limp puppy. She stretched out, panting, as Timmy and Boomer gave the puppy first aid.

It took only a couple of minutes of massaging and pumping water out and breath into the tiny body, before the puppy gave a faint, protesting yip at the rough treatment.

'He's okay!' Boomer exclaimed triumphantly.

Timmy nodded. The puppy staggered to its feet, and went weaving over to Lassie. Then he crawled between her outstretched paws, curled up, and gave every sign that he intended to stay in that friendly haven. And Lassie licked the wet, cold little body in the gentlest way, till the puppy had stopped shivering and was asleep.

'I thought Letty'd be with Pom-Pom,' Timmy sighed.

'Maybe he was lookin' for her, too. Same as us an' the sheriff,' Boomer suggested.

Timmy pointed to some marks in the mud and sand at the edge of the path along the creek. 'Hey! That looks like Taffy's hoofprints!' he told Boomer.

Boomer went over to look, and stepped on the same soft and treacherous piece of ground that Taffy had struggled against. 'Yipe!' he yelled, waving his arms and grabbing at a bush to keep himself from sliding down the bank into the fast-moving water.

And as Timmy dashed over to lend a hand, he saw something familiar lying on the ground a couple of feet from the soft edge. He stopped abruptly, staring.

It was one of Letty's riding gloves.

'Gimme a hand!' Boomer was hanging on to that bush for dear life, and any moment he might have to let go and fall into the water – while his best friend stopped to gawk at something! 'Hurry up!'

But, instead, Timmy picked up the glove, and stood staring at it with a dazed look on his face. 'It's hers, all right!' he told himself. 'She an' Taffy must've fallen in, about here. An' Taffy got out an' ran home – ' he stared out into the rushing water as if he expected to see

Letty there, and then finished in a whisper as the full meaning of the evidence struck him suddenly, ' – but – I guess she – she's still there . . . '

Boomer had managed to catch hold of another, higher bush with his free hand, and was valiantly hauling himself out. He yelled crossly at Timmy, 'Help me, won't you?' but Timmy was standing looking out at the creek with a strange expression on his face, and didn't seem to hear him at all.

Boomer was almost up to dry ground, on the slippery bank. Then as he tugged at the higher bush, its roots gave way, and he started to slide backwards down the bank. He gave a terrified yell.

Lassie got up quickly, but carefully so she wouldn't disturb the round ball of white fur sleeping between her paws. And when she had backed off from the puppy, she trotted over to the very edge of the bank above Boomer, leaned over and grabbed him by the back of his sweater. Then, bracing herself, she started backing away and at the same time hauling Boomer up, an inch at a time.

It was hard on the sweater, but it held Boomer from dropping down into the swirling water. He yelled angrily at Timmy, 'Hurry up! What's the matter with you?' as he tried to help Lassie help him. And Timmy snapped out of his daze enough to run over at last, and pull him up the final couple of feet to safety.

When Boomer was sure that he was really safe, he yelled tearfully at Timmy, 'Why didn't you come when I called? I mighta drowned!'

Timmy looked at him wide-eyed, and showed him Letty's glove. 'I found this in the mud. I guess maybe Letty was riding Taffy when he fell into the water.'

143

Boomer's ruddy face was several shades paler as he stared at the glove, and then looked quickly out at the turbulent creek waters. 'Maybe she could swim. Maybe she's okay.'

Timmy shook his head solemnly. 'She couldn't swim. Her dad was going to teach her' – his voice broke – 'this summer!'

Lassie barked suddenly. She had heard something that they hadn't heard yet. She stood facing the road and barking excitedly.

'Maybe it's Letty! Maybe she did get out okay! Hey, Letty! It's us! Me an' Boomer!' Timmy yelled excitedly.

'Where are you?' Boomer shrieked. Then he remembered the whistle, and gave several shrill blasts on it. If she was anywhere within half a mile, she would hear *that*!

But it wasn't Letty who answered the whistle. It was Paul Martin. He ran towards them through the brush, with Uncle Petrie and one of the deputies at his heels.

'Timmy! Boomer! What are you doing here?' He frowned, looking around quickly for Letty. 'Have you found Letty?'

'No, sir,' Timmy answered sadly, 'but we found this.' He handed over the glove. 'It's hers.'

'And there's Taffy's hoofprints. That's where he fell into the water!' Boomer pointed. 'I near fell in, myself, just now. I woulda drowned if Lassie hadn't held on to me, I bet!'

The three men exchanged quick looks as they examined the slippery bank. The pony could have slipped . . . the saddle could have twisted . . . and Letty could have been thrown into the flooding creek . . .

'Boys, I think you'd better take Lassie on home now,' Paul told them, trying to keep his voice light. 'We don't want to worry your mothers. And Boomer needs some dry clothes anyhow.'

'But Lassie can help you find Letty!' Timmy argued.

'Timmy!' Paul said sternly. 'Do as I say! And get started right away.'

The puppy was staggering around sleepily. 'One of you had better carry that pup!' Uncle Petrie suggested. 'Here, I'll show you how!'

He made a carrying sling of Timmy's jacket and tied it around Timmy's neck, hanging down in front. The puppy snuggled down quite comfortably in it, with only his small fluffy white head and his bright little eyes visible.

The two boys trudged off, much against their wishes.

Lassie, as usual, led the way as they went through the woods towards the road. But every now and again she stopped and gazed back in the direction they had come.

'See?' Timmy pouted. 'Lassie doesn't want to go home! Her feelin's are hurt because Dad wouldn't let her help find Letty!'

'I bet they'd all feel silly if we did find her!' Boomer said bitterly. Then his eyes widened. 'Say, why don't we do like you said, and go ask old Joey if he's seen her?'

'But Dad said to go home!' Timmy always tried to be obedient, even if it was a strain.

'Oh, okay!' Boomer looked scornful, 'but it wouldn't take long to get to the cave, if we started right now. Then if Joey says he hasn't seen her, we can go straight home.'

10

Timmy squirmed. 'But it looks like she fell in the creek. I could tell Dad thinks so, too, the way he got rid of us!'

'Well, s'pose she did fall in!' Boomer scowled. 'That don't mean she couldn't climb out again some place along the creek, does it? 'Specially if she wasn't hurt much.'

'Yeah!' Timmy looked happy for the first time in hours.

'Well? How about it?' Boomer still wanted to make the decisions and be the hero.

'Okay. Let's go!' Timmy agreed. And they started off hastily by a very faint trail that was their special short cut through the thick woods to the cave.

Sheriff Bennett and his other deputy had crisscrossed the woods, and were starting for the brush-filled ravines beyond, when they heard the single pistol shot that told them that Paul and the others had found something. They doubled back to a meeting beside the creek.

'It looks bad, at that,' Sheriff Bennett agreed grimly, after examining the evidence of the hoofprints and the lost glove. 'I'm afraid that when we do find her . . .' He didn't need to finish it. The men could do that for themselves, unhappily!

They set out to search the creek banks as far as the first bend, a mile downstream. Things often washed ashore there, after a storm.

19

Home Again

Letty had been napping, curled up in the shade of the big sun-dappled rock. At first, she had cried a little about being lost and hungry, but the sun-warmed breeze had soon lulled her to sleep.

She hadn't felt brave enough to try to find her way home out of the big dark woods. Besides, she was afraid she might see the big man with the dead rabbits over his shoulder. He looked like a story-book ogre!

A distant revolver shot made her stir, and then suddenly she was wide awake. Something had touched her, and even now was nudging her shoulder. She was almost too scared to look, but then she heard a familiar little whimper, and she knew that a friend had found her.

It was Lassie, watching her with bright brown eyes, and now, putting a slim paw on her lap in greeting.

'Oh, Lassie! I'm so glad to see you!' Letty squeezed her so hard with both arms that Lassie hardly had enough breath left to bark. But she managed somehow! And she kept on barking.

A hundred feet away on the other side of a thicket, Timmy and Boomer were pushing along on their trail to the cave when they heard Lassie barking.

Timmy stopped abruptly. 'Hey! She's found something! And she sounds like it's something she likes!'

Pom-Pom, riding peacefully up to now in the coat sling that Uncle Petrie had fixed up, seemed to hear something good, too, in Lassie's barking. He struggled to get out of the sling, and before Timmy could stop him he had leaped to the ground and run off in the direction of the barking. His own shrill yipping as he ran answered the deep wroofing of Lassie.

'Come on! Let's see!' Timmy yelled to Boomer, and immediately plunged into the bushes to follow the poodle. Boomer was close on his heels.

When Timmy came rushing through the brush, he was astonished and delighted to see Letty, looking quite calm and serene on her rock, one arm around Lassie and the other around Pom-Pom, who was doing his best to tell Letty in his usual wildly enthusiastic way that he was delighted to see her again.

'Hi, Letty!' Timmy shouted. 'We been lookin' all over for you! Are you okay?'

Boomer followed Timmy through the brush. 'Hey, we thought you got drowned!'

Letty reassured them both, and then, after looking them both over eagerly, asked, 'Didn't you bring along something to eat? I'm awfully hungry!'

'Eat?' They exchanged baffled looks. They hadn't thought about eating. They suddenly realised that they were hungry, themselves.

148

Then Timmy had a bright idea. 'Maybe Joey has something to eat at the cave. We're only a little ways from there, and he'll be glad to give you some of his food!'

'Joey?' She frowned. 'Who's that?'

'A nice old man, a friend of mine,' Timmy explained.

Letty asked abruptly, 'Does he have a black beard – an' big, big feet? An' does he shoot rabbits?'

The boys looked startled. 'He has a beard, but it's grey,' Timmy told her. 'I never noticed his feet. But he wouldn't shoot a rabbit for anything, I know. He loves them, and they're all friends of his!'

Letty let out her breath in a sigh of relief. 'That's good. Let's go.'

Boomer frowned. 'Whatcha wanta know about his feet for?'

Letty showed them the footprints that the black-bearded stranger had left when he passed earlier.

When she had finished telling them about him, Timmy said positively, 'That wasn't Joey. He's real nice.'

So they started off, three hungry ones. Lassie led the procession, with Pom-Pom frisking at her heels.

But their reception at the cave was to be anything but the friendly one that Timmy and Boomer were expecting.

For the last hour, the real Blackie Sanders had been sleeping. He had gorged himself on the rabbit stew, and then packed what was left of it into old Joey's cooking tin. 'This I take along,' he had told Joey.

'But it's all I got for cooking,' Joey protested.

Blackie laughed harshly. 'Seeing there ain't much

149

here to cook, hobo, that don't seem to make much difference.'

The news that this black-bearded, mean-eyed man was the real escaped convict, and that *he* was still the nameless wanderer, had brought a measure of relief to old Joey. But if he wasn't Sanders, who was he? Just a homeless tramp, going nowhere? But where, then, was the hospital that he was so sure he could remember, even if all the rest was a blank? And why had he been there?

He was puzzling unhappily over his problem, when he heard Timmy's voice calling, 'Mister Joey!'

He stole a quick look towards the corner where Blackie was sleeping. The big man hadn't moved.

Joey started moving hastily towards the cave mouth. He would send Timmy away, before Blackie could wake up and maybe frighten the boy.

But he was only halfway to the entrance of the cave, when Blackie snarled, 'Hold it, hobo!' and Joey saw that he had risen and was striding towards him.

Joey wanted to run out and away, but the look in the black-beard's eye stopped him. He explained lamely, 'It's one of the little kids. I'll chase him away. He might tell his pa there's two of us here now, if he saw you.'

Blackie grinned crookedly. 'Yeah, and *you* just might be figuring to slip him the word who the other guy is!'

'I won't tell him, honest!' Joey protested.

'I know you won't!' the big man snarled. 'Because I don't figure to let you!'

'Joey! Yoo-hoo! Are you in there?' Timmy was calling, and Boomer's voice added, 'Aw, I bet he ran away a long time ago! He was just a tramp!'

'He was not!' Timmy's voice was shrill. 'He was my

friend. An' I'm going in an' look for him. Maybe he's sick!'

'Okay, chase 'em away!' Blackie snapped. 'But don't try to give 'em any messages. I'll be watching!' He patted the gun in his belt. 'Play it cool!'

'I'm coming,' Joey called out, a little shakily.

'He *is* there!' Timmy's voice shouted.

Joey was still a few feet inside the cave, when his foot struck the cartridge box that Blackie had stolen from Sam Moss's store in Calverton. It was empty now, and Blackie had discarded it. Joey scowled at it and gave it a kick ahead of him and out into the sunlight.

At sight of him, Timmy and Boomer started to hurry towards the mouth of the cave, with Letty a close third. But Lassie held back. The hair on the back of her neck stood up, and she growled as she stared at the cave.

Joey stopped the boys as they scrambled towards him. 'Don't come in here!' he called out, trying to make it as harsh as he could. 'I don't want you young'uns hanging around here any more. You git! And don't come back!'

Timmy was astonished. He could hardly believe his ears. His friendly old man was scowling and motioning for them to go. 'Hey, it's *us*!' he called out weakly to Joey.

Boomer's face got red, and he glared defiantly at Joey. 'We don't have to go if we don't wanta!' he said sassily. 'It was our cave first, an' *you* better move out, or I'll tell the sheriff!'

'Scoot! Get away from here!' Joey shouted. 'I ain't leaving here! Tell anybody you like!' and he shook a threatening fist at them.

'Yah!' Boomer made a face. 'Ol' tramp!' He held his

ground impudently. 'Who's afraid of you?'

But Timmy and Letty were not so bold. 'Let's go back,' Timmy said. 'Come on.' He tugged at Boomer's sleeve.

Lassie, who had put herself between Timmy and old Joey, growled and showed her teeth, but she didn't jump at Joey. And then Timmy noticed that she was looking past Joey and snarling at something deep in the cave.

'Git, I say!' Joey picked up the empty cartridge box and flung it towards them.

The empty box struck Boomer on the arm, and fell to the ground at his feet. Angrily, he picked it up and was about to throw it back at the old man, when they all heard a loud sneeze from inside the cave. Boomer's arm dropped to his side, but he still unconsciously held on to the empty shell box. 'Hey, what was that?' he asked Timmy, with a puzzled frown. 'Sounded like a sneeze!'

Timmy thought so, too. Lassie was still staring at something in the cave that was bothering her – and Timmy felt pretty sure that whatever it was, it had sneezed. And it was a man-sized sneeze! He said hastily, 'Let's get outa here!' and with that, he grabbed Letty's arm, and started hurrying her away from the cave. 'Come on, Boomer!'

Boomer hesitated only an instant, then he turned and fled after them, almost tripping over Pom-Pom, who was racing after Timmy and Letty and barking gaily.

Lassie was the only one who held her ground, snarling past Joey at the man in the dark recess of the cave. She was Timmy's rear guard now, and she wouldn't move till he called her to come.

'Shoo, Lassie!' Joey waved his arm at her urgently.

But she waited until, to Joey's relief, she heard Timmy call from a distance, 'Come, Lassie! Lassie!' Then she backed a few steps watchfully, wheeled, and ran off.

Joey was shaking as he went back into the cave. 'I drove 'em off,' he told Sanders sullenly.

Then he busied himself cleaning up, puttering in the back of the cave. He felt sure Sanders hadn't noticed him throw the stolen cartridge box at the boy. Now, if the boy would do as he said, and go to the sheriff, they might come looking –

Almost as if he had read Joey's mind, Sanders said, suddenly, 'I'm pulling out by sundown. Too many people around all of a sudden.'

Timmy and Boomer helped Letty through the tangled brush, and the two dogs followed. But Letty was too tired to go far. 'You go on,' she told the boys bravely.

'Nothin' doin',' Timmy said fiercely. 'We're not leaving you!' Then he sat down to wait for her to rest, much to Boomer's annoyance. Boomer wanted to get out of there.

Lassie suddenly started barking loudly. A moment later, they heard Paul Martin shouting in answer, 'Timmy! Lassie! Where are you?'

Then all three yelled at once. A few minutes later, Paul Martin, Uncle Petrie, Dave Brunson and several others, found them.

Sheriff Bennett and Paul were so delighted to see Letty safe and well, that they didn't pay much attention to the excited report from the boys, about the stranger in the cave.

But all of a sudden, Sam Moss noticed the cartridge box in Boomer's hand, and recognised it as the one

153

that had been stolen from him. He showed it to the others excitedly.

'Where is this cave?' Paul asked Timmy.

'We'll show you,' Timmy volunteered, but Boomer didn't want to go back there. He wanted to go home. He had had enough excitement for one day.

'Timmy, you and Lassie can lead us, while Uncle Petrie takes Letty and Boomer home,' Paul suggested.

That suited everyone, and Uncle Petrie was soon on his way, carrying Letty on his shoulder, and with Pom-Pom and Boomer tagging after.

When they got in sight of the cave, Paul told Timmy to stay back, in case of trouble with Joey and his unknown companion. But Timmy was worried about old Joey, and he tagged along, with Lassie, against orders.

There were three of them, Sheriff Bennett, Paul, and Sam Moss, as they went cautiously towards the dark mouth of the cave. They were making as little noise as possible, but Blackie Sanders had already heard them, and was waiting just inside the cave, gun in hand.

The first man within range would be his target.

Joey saw them coming, and knew what was going to happen. At the last moment, he flung himself at Blackie's gunhand, and tried to disarm the convict.

But Blackie had expected something like that, and he knocked the old man away from him with a powerful blow of his fist. Joey staggered and collapsed in the dirt.

The men outside, hearing the struggle, rushed forward, and Blackie turned his revolver towards them. Paul Martin was in the lead, moving fast. In another second he would be in easy range. Blackie cocked his revolver, but as he did, something struck his arm.

It was Lassie, a snarling, growling bundle of fury.

Before Blackie could get over his surprise and turn the revolver on her, she had knocked him down, and had fastened her teeth in his wrist, pulling and tearing at it till his fingers relaxed. He dropped the gun and yowled.

Paul ran forward, swept up the gun, and levelled it at the convict. He called off Lassie. 'All right, girl! We've got him now!' he told her.

The handcuffs were soon on Sanders's wrists. He was angry and defiant. 'You never woulda had a chance,' he boasted, 'if that goofy old guy hadn't jumped me. And this cur – ' He glared at Lassie, who curled her lip up over her teeth and glared back. Blackie decided to say no more!

'Mister Joey!' Timmy ran into the cave. Then they heard him yell, 'Dad! Mr Bennett! Please come quick!'

They found him kneeling beside the unconscious Joey.

'Please do somethin' for Joey!' he pleaded. 'He's hurt!'

The men stared down at the grey-bearded stranger. 'He looks sort of familiar,' Sam Moss said, frowning.

Joey was starting to come to, now. Timmy and Paul leaned over him. 'Mister Joey! Are you all right?' Timmy asked anxiously.

And as Paul helped the old man to sit up, he looked at them with surprise. 'Who – who are you? Where am I?'

Suddenly Sam Moss remembered. 'Joe Brunson!' He leaned over. 'Joe! It's me, Sam Moss! And you're home in Calverton!'

Recognition dawned in Joey's eyes. 'Sam! What's

been going on? How did I get here?'

That was a question that was answered within a few days. Joe Brunson had had a head injury during the war, and had lost his memory completely.

For several years he had drifted from one government hospital to another, taking treatments, but failing to remember anything of his past. Then one day he had run away, and instinctively had drifted to the old valley where he, his wife, and his boy had spent a few happy years.

Letty was proud and delighted to have a grandfather, and Dave to have a father again. Dave's only regret was that they would still have to give up the farm. Several people wanted to buy it, and even with his father's farming ability, they would have to sell it to live.

But they were due for a happy surprise the very day before they had planned to move.

Thanks to the testimony of those who were at the taking of Sanders, the reward for his capture went to Joe Brunson, who in addition had undoubtedly saved Paul Martin's life by his reckless attack on the armed convict.

The reward money would enable them to stay on at the farm, and be happy. And it also gave them a chance to do something to show Timmy how much they appreciated Lassie's help through it all.

The something was a wonderful leather collar, with a metal tag on it. The engraving on the tag said, TO LASSIE, THE BRAVEST EVER.

And from the way Lassie strutted when she wore it, Timmy almost decided that maybe she *could* read. It seemed quite possible, considering everything else she had done!

156

TARGET STORY BOOKS

Adventure

Gordon Boshell
113918 **THE BLACK MERCEDES** 60p

114043 **THE MILLION POUND RANSOM** 60p

117468 **THE MENDIP MONEY-MAKERS** 60p

Animal Stories

Molly Burkett
118502 **FOXES, OWLS AND ALL** (NF) (illus) 70p

111567 **THAT MAD, BAD BADGER ...** (NF) (illus) 35p

Constance Taber Colby
109899 **A SKUNK IN THE FAMILY** (NF) (illus) 45p

I. J. Edmonds
20011X **LASSIE: THE WILD MOUNTAIN TRAIL** 60p

G. D. Griffiths
113675 **ABANDONED!** (illus) 50p

David Gross
117549 **THE BADGERS OF BADGER HILL** (illus) 50p

Michael Maguire
118774 **MYLOR, THE MOST POWERFUL HORSE IN THE WORLD** (illus) 60p

Joyce Stranger
11017X **THE SECRET HERDS** (illus) 45p

110099 **THE HARE AT DARK HOLLOW** (illus) 40p

Mystery And Suspense

Ruth M. Arthur
111648 **THE AUTUMN GHOSTS** (illus) 50p

111729 **THE CANDLEMAS MYSTERY** (illus) 45p*

Tim Dinsdale
105915 **THE STORY OF THE LOCH NESS MONSTER** (illus) 50p

Leonard Gribble
104285 **FAMOUS HISTORICAL MYSTERIES** (NF) (illus) 50p

Alfred Hitchcock (Editor)
117387 **ALFRED HITCHCOCK'S TALES OF TERROR AND SUSPENSE** 60p

Mollie Hunter
113756 **THE WALKING STONES** (illus) 45p*†

Freya Littledale
107357 **GHOSTS AND SPIRITS OF MANY LANDS** (illus) 50p

†For sale in Britain and Ireland only.
*Not for sale in Canada.
♦ Film & T.V. tie-ins.

TARGET STORY BOOKS

Fantasy And General Fiction

101537	Elisabeth Beresford **AWKWARD MAGIC**	(illus)	60p
10479X	**SEA-GREEN MAGIC**	(illus)	60p
101618	**TRAVELLING MAGIC**	(illus)	60p
119142	Eileen Dunlop **ROBINSHEUGH**	(illus)	60p
112288	Maria Gripe **THE GLASSBLOWER'S CHILDREN**	(illus)	45p
117891	Joyce Nicholson **FREEDOM FOR PRISCILLA**		70p
106989	Hilary Seton **THE HUMBLES**	(illus)	50p
109112	**THE NOEL STREATFEILD CHRISTMAS HOLIDAY BOOK**	(illus)	60p
109031	**THE NOEL STREATFEILD EASTER HOLIDAY BOOK**	(illus)	60p
105249	**THE NOEL STREATFEILD SUMMER HOLIDAY BOOK**	(illus)	50p

Humour

107519	Eleanor Estes **THE WITCH FAMILY**	(illus)	50p
11762X	Felice Holman **THE WITCH ON THE CORNER**	(illus)	50p
105672	Spike Milligan **BADJELLY THE WITCH**	(illus)	60p
109546	**DIP THE PUPPY**	(illus)	60p
107438	Christine Nostlinger **THE CUCUMBER KING**	(illus)	45p
119223	Mary Rogers **A BILLION FOR BORIS**		60p

0426 Film And TV Tie-ins

200187	Kathleen N. Daly **RAGGEDY ANN AND ANDY** (Colour illus)		75p ♦
11826X	John Ryder Hall **SINBAD AND THE EYE OF THE TIGER**		70p* ♦
11535X	John Lucarotti **OPERATION PATCH**		45p
119495	Pat Sandys **THE PAPER LADS**		60p ♦
115511	Alison Thomas **BENJI**		40p

† For sale in Britain and Ireland only.
* Not for sale in Canada.
♦ Film & T.V. tie-ins.

TARGET NON-FICTION

General Non-fiction
And biography

Quiz And Games

Wyndham Books are obtainable from many booksellers and newsagents. If you have any difficulty please send purchase price plus postage on the scale below to:

Wyndham Cash Sales:
P O Box 11,
Falmouth,
Cornwall.

or

Star Book Service:
G P O Box 29,
Douglas,
Isle of Man,
British Isles.

While every effort is made to keep prices low, it is sometimes necessary to increase prices at short notice. Wyndham Books reserve the right to show new retail prices on covers which may differ from those advertised in the text or elsewhere.

Postage and Packing Rate
UK
22p for the first book plus 10p per copy for each additional book ordered to a maximum charge of 82p.

BFPO and Eire
22p for the first book, plus 10p per copy for the next 6 books and thereafter 4p per book.

Overseas
30p for the first book and 10p per copy for each additional book.

These charges are subject to Post Office charge fluctuations.